gorilla dawn

gorilla dawn

by Gill Lewis

Illustrated by
Susan Meyer

SCHOLASTIC INC.

Originally published in Great Britain in 2015 by Oxford University Press

ISBN 978-1-338-27791-3

12 11 10 9 8 7 6 5 4 3 2 1   18 19 20 21 22 23

Printed in the U.S.A.   40

First Scholastic printing, January 2018

Book design by Sonia Chaghatzbanian
The text for this book was set in Garamond.
The illustrations for this book were digitally rendered.

To the thin green line:
The men and women rangers who risk their lives
protecting wildlife and wild places for us all.

gorilla dawn

In the east of the Democratic Republic of Congo lie areas of forested wilderness that are home to the eastern lowland gorilla. Beneath the canopy, the forests support an extraordinary diversity of life, from rare plants to forest elephants. Yet, beneath the soil, they have the highest concentration of mineral resources found anywhere on earth; minerals that continue to fuel internal conflict and world greed.

These forests drive our global weather patterns. They regulate the air we breathe and the water we drink. They give life to those living on the forests' edges and those who live thousands of miles away.

They are essential to us all.

And yet, they are at risk of being lost forever.

These forests are where this story begins. . . .

"When we try to pick out anything by itself, we find it hitched to everything else in the universe."
John Muir (1838–1914)

PART ONE

then . . .

YOU ARE MINE, IMARA.

THE DAY THEY CUT YOU OPEN,
I CLIMBED INSIDE.
KEEP ME SAFE IN HERE, AND I WILL
MAKE YOU STRONG.
IF YOU LET ME OUT, THEY WILL SEE
YOUR WEAKNESS AND YOU WILL DIE.
YOU CANNOT LIVE WITH ME, YET YOU
CANNOT SURVIVE WITHOUT ME.

YOU ARE MINE, IMARA.
YOU ARE THE DEVIL'S CHILD.

CHAPTER ONE

imara

*I*t is time, Imara.

Imara left the shadows and stepped into the pool of moonlight, listening to the demon as he paced inside her mind.

It is time, Imara. The men are waiting for you. They are waiting for your power to protect them.

She knelt down and poured the contents of her water bottle into the ashes of last night's fire, stirring with her fingers, working the mixture into a gritty paste.

All around her, the forest was dark and still,

wrapped in silence. Nothing moved. High above in the canopy, a pale mist clung to the leaves. Thin tendrils of vapor hung in the air, as if the trees were holding their breath, waiting for the dawn.

The Black Mamba and his men were folded into the deep moon-shadows. Only the cold light catching the metal of their rifles told they were not of this place.

Come on, Imara, hissed the demon. **They're watching you.**

Imara's hands hovered over the ash paste and trembled.

Stupid girl. Don't show your fear. You know what they'll do if they see your fear.

Imara breathed in deeply, filling her lungs with the cool night air. She tried to block her mind from the purpose of her task. She hummed softly, trying to ignore the demon and scooped the ash paste into her hand.

Hurry, Imara. They want to see their spirit child.

She worked faster, scraping more wet ash from the middle of the fire, squeezing it in her fists, letting the water run out between her fingers. She began to smear the ash paste, covering the raised scar that cut her face in two. She traced its hard ragged surface from her forehead, across her cheek to her lower jaw. The scar had long since healed, sealing the demon deep inside, but its tightness pulled her mouth into a twisted scowl.

She could feel the ash mixture dry and harden like a shell. Next, she smeared the ash paste on her bare arms, painting long sinuous bodies of snakes from her shoulders to her wrists. As the ash dried, it glowed white in the moonlight, bright against her dark skin.

The Black Mamba stepped out from the trees. He was a big man, thick-necked, like a bull buffalo. His anger was unpredictable like one, too. He rolled up his sleeve and thrust his arm in front of Imara. Her eyes came to rest on the snake-bone amulet around his wrist, the snake from which the Black

Mamba took his name. "Protect me, Imara," he whispered.

Imara dipped her fingers into the ash and traced a snake along his forearm, curling the tail into a spiral. "It is done," she said. "The spirits will look after you. No one can harm you now."

The Black Mamba nodded and stood up. "Now safeguard my men."

The men lined up to have their arms painted with her dark magic, but none of them dared look Imara in the eye. She was the Black Mamba's Spirit Child. She talked with the devil and walked within the spirit world. The spirits protected her. She had been bitten by a black mamba and lived.

"Come," said the Black Mamba. He held up his arm, the ash snake glowing bright in the darkness. "It is time to take back what is ours."

Imara followed the Black Mamba and his men to the forest edge. She squeezed her eyes tight shut and gripped the barrel of her gun, the metal cold against her skin. She focused on the sounds of the

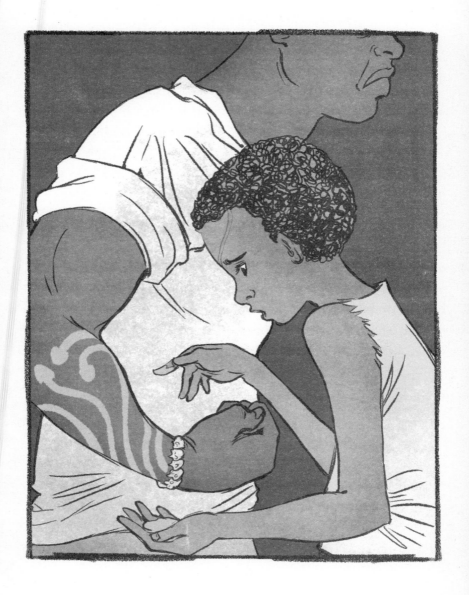

waking forest, on the leaves rippling in a fresh breeze above her and the chorus of birds. She tried to control her breathing, slowing her breath so she could taste the damp, earthy air. She tried to ignore the demon kicking inside her chest.

But the demon would not be quiet.

Open your eyes, Imara.

The demon beat his fists against her chest. *Thump . . . thump . . . thump.*

Open your eyes, Imara! They are not like us. They are weak. They deserve to die.

Imara forced her eyes open and stared down to the village in the valley below. The sun had not yet risen above the mountains. Small fires flickered in the pale dawn light. Villagers moved between the huts, the reds and yellows of women's skirts bright in the blue mist of early morning. The bleats of goats and the steady pounding of cassava carried up the hillside. Wood smoke drifted across the fields bringing the smell of roasting corn to the forest edge where Imara crouched, concealed in darkness.

She made a circle with her finger and thumb, and held it to her eye. She looked through to see the village, cupping it within her hand. She tried to hold the image, as if she could somehow protect it in her memory, protect the villagers from what was to come.

But it was a new day.

A new dawn.

On the eastern horizon, a crimson light was bleeding into the sky. The villagers below were unaware of the girl at the edge of the forest, the girl with a gun and necklace of bullets. They were unaware of the Black Mamba and his men beside her. Unaware many of them would not live to see the sun rising above the mountains.

CHAPTER TWO

imara

The Black Mamba rapped his fingers on his gun. "Are we being watched, Imara? Do they know we are here?"

Imara scanned the fields beyond for tell-tale glowing cigarette ends of men hiding out in the fields, ready for an ambush. But the fields were quiet and still.

"We have not been seen," she said.

Even in the darkness, Imara could feel the Black Mamba's presence. "There is no one guarding this village," she said. "But see how fat the cattle are.

These people have kinship with the land here. They won't give it up easily."

The Black Mamba breathed out slowly. "It is not *their* land. They stole it from us when they fled their homes in Rwanda. This is Congo soil. This is our land."

Imara heard thirty rifles release their safety catches in agreement. She looked along the line of trees at the forest edge. The Black Mamba's men were hidden in the shadows. Waiting. Invisible. Only the sour smell of their sweat gave them away.

"Come," said the Black Mamba to his men. He touched the snake-bone amulet on his wrist. "Let us take back what is ours." He stepped out from the shadows and paused. "Rat," he called. "Where are you?" A wiry man with strands of hair braided like rats' tails slunk out of the forest to stand beside him. "Rat, you stay with Imara. Let nothing harm our Spirit Child. She gives us our strength and keeps us safe. It is she who turns enemy bullets into rain."

Imara sank back farther into the shadows and

watched the Black Mamba's men spread out across the fields. They moved silently down through the rows of corn.

The demon beat his fists, drumming out a war song, faster and faster.

Rat was tense beside her, his finger twitching on the trigger of his gun, his eyes focused on the valley. Imara could hear the grinding of his teeth on the wad of dagga in his mouth. She could see the wildness in his eyes as it infused his mind.

In the valley, a dog barked, breaking the silence.

Imara pushed her fingers in her ears to block out the coming battle. She wanted to run and run, and be anywhere but here. But there was nowhere to run. The Mambas would only track her down.

Rat's staccato laughter rang out with the first round of gunfire. "Watch them run, Imara. They look so funny when they run. See their feet flying high up in the air. Look at the mamas with children clinging to them like baboon babies."

Imara squinted through half-closed eyes. She

saw figures running out across the fields and others strewn like rags across the ground. She saw the orange flare of shots where the Black Mamba's men hunted the villagers down. A boy's high-pitched cry was silenced by gunfire. Imara turned her face into the forest. She hated to hear the children die.

Rat spat on the ground beside her. "Don't pity the cubs, Imara. They become the lions that will hunt you down."

Imara watched him from the shadows. He was fueled with excitement, jogging on the spot. She knew he wanted to be fighting in the valley, taking his share of the food. Taking his share of the glory.

He glanced in her direction, avoiding her eyes. "Stay here," he said. "Don't show yourself until I return." He slung his rifle across his shoulder and headed off to join the battle.

Imara curled herself into a ball. She tried to tell herself she wasn't part of this nightmare, but the demon twisted Imara's stomach. **Don't pretend you aren't hungry, Imara. You haven't eaten for days.**

The men will return with food, much food. Didn't you hear the Black Mamba? This is our land. Our food. We are taking back what is ours.

The demon laughed wildly as the first hut burst into flames, the straw roof sending up a plume of thick smoke. Imara could see the silhouettes of the Black Mamba and his men heading back toward the forest. They were laden with sacks. Two men each carried a live goat across their shoulders. At the end of the line of men walked three boys, pushed forward by Rat.

The Black Mamba reached the forest edge puffing and sweating. The veins on his neck stood out like cords of rope. "You were right," he said to Imara. "They tried to fight us. We lost three of our men." He wiped blood from the long blade of his panga on the grass. "So we have taken three of theirs."

Imara watched the three boys stumble into the middle of the ring formed by the Black Mamba's men. They were soot- and tear-stained. The acrid smell of smoke clung to their clothes.

The first boy was tall and gangly, with wide, staring eyes.

The Black Mamba faced him. "How old?"

The boy stared ahead, unable to form words inside his mouth. His cheeks sucked in and out. In and out. His eyes bulged wide open.

The Black Mamba held the boy's cheeks tightly in one hand and laughed. "This is not a boy . . . it is a frog!" He turned to his men. "We have caught a frog!"

The Mambas laughed. They were in a good mood. Rat chewed on a roasted corn, still warm from one of the village fires.

The second boy was shorter, about Imara's height. He had sharp, quick eyes.

"And you? How old are you?"

"Twelve," said the boy.

"What is your name?"

"Dikembe."

"Well, Dikembe, you are old enough to be a man. Can you fight?"

The boy nodded.

The Black Mamba pushed the handle of his panga toward Dikembe. "Would you kill him for us?" he said, pointing to the third boy. "Would you kill him?"

Dikembe nodded. He held the panga, although it shook uncontrollably in his hand.

The Black Mamba laughed and took back his panga. "And you," he said, turning to the third boy. "What good are you to us?"

Rat pushed the boy to the ground. "This one is a Batwa. A pygmy."

Imara watched the boy struggle back to his feet. He was small and skinny, no taller than the Black Mamba's gun. At first she had thought he was a young child, but his face was that of an older boy.

The boy jutted his chin forward. "My name is Saka."

The Black Mamba circled around the boy, coming to a stop in front of him. He bent down, their faces inches apart. "What is a pygmy doing in this village?"

"We should kill him now," said Rat. He spat on the ground. "The pygmies are no better than animals."

The Black Mamba scratched at the bristles of a beard on his chin and turned to Imara. "Let the Spirit Child decide."

Imara turned toward the boys. She could see them staring at her scar and twisted face. Her eyes fixed on the small Batwa boy. He returned her gaze from big brown eyes. She didn't see fear in him, but an acceptance of what was to come. She could feel the pain deep in her chest of the demon twisting her heart round and round and round.

Don't pity him, Imara. Don't give in to your weakness. Only the strong survive.

"Well?" said the Black Mamba. "What do the spirits say? Does the boy live or die?"

"Kill him," insisted Rat. He shoved Saka in the chest. "You are stupid. Useless. An animal."

Imara clenched her fists, digging her nails into her skin. She tried to block out the demon's voice but it cried louder and louder into her ear.

The boy must die.

The boy must die.

The boy must die.

CHAPTER THREE

imara

"Well, Imara? What do we do with him?"

The Black Mamba was waiting for his answer. He pushed his panga against the boy's chest, the tip of the long blade pressing into his skin.

The small boy looked up at Imara with unblinking eyes. No one else dared look directly at her. All men feared her. She was the one who spoke with the devil. She had the power to curse a man's soul. To look into her eyes was to see your own death, yet this boy dared. He stared as if he could see right inside her, forcing her to look away.

He will find your weakness, hissed the demon. **The boy must die.**

Gunfire broke through Imara's thoughts and shattered the silence. In the valley below, the headlights of two trucks bumped across the dirt tracks. Orange flares lit the sky.

Rat pointed at the dark shadows of men making their way up the hillside. "Government troops," he said. "They must have been waiting for us on the other side of the valley. Look, they outnumber us."

"Traitors!" The Black Mamba swore beneath his breath. "Come, they won't follow us into the forest." He turned to Imara. "Protect the men."

Imara carved a snake into the bark of the nearest tree, dark magic to ward people away. Rat stood beside her, pointing his rifle at the small boy, thirsty for a kill.

"No," said Imara, pushing the barrel of Rat's gun away.

Rat scowled. "Why? You don't pity him, do you?"

"No," spat Imara. "But he may be useful. Let

him live for now. I will decide his fate later."

The Black Mamba nodded. "Let's go."

Imara could feel Rat's eyes burning into her.

The demon crawled in her ear. **Be careful, Imara. Rat hates you. He's jealous of your power over the Black Mamba. He wants to find a way to bring you down. Show him you don't care for the boy.**

Imara scowled and gave Saka a hard shove. "Walk," she ordered. "Or I shoot."

She followed the men into the forest, along the paths they had hacked through the undergrowth the night before. Rat and two other Mambas fired at the government troops from the safety of the trees, giving the Black Mamba and the rest of his men time to slip away.

Imara chewed on a piece of corn as she walked, sucking the last sweetness out of the hard cob. The mud was soft and sticky beneath her feet. Her boots were soaked, the hard leather rubbing a new blister on her heel. Tiredness swept over her. She had marched through the previous night and it was unlikely she would sleep until they made camp in the evening. The men were tired too. All she could hear were their grunts and labored breathing as they made their way through the forest. They looked like exhausted men, not the feared Mambas.

Rumors of the Mambas told of men who could walk for days and nights without food or sleep. They could pass unseen through the forests. Invisible. Invincible. If one Mamba was killed, two more rose up to take his place. They had a secret weapon to protect them, too. Imara. She was their Spirit Child. She gave them their power.

Imara looked up at the sky to catch glimpses of the sun beyond the canopy of leaves. The Black Mamba was moving his men eastward through the lowlands toward the mountains. He had promised them the greatest prize, a land of plenty. A land to make them rich.

She glanced back at Saka, half wishing Rat had killed him sooner and got it over and done with.

Surely the small boy wouldn't be able to keep up with the march through the forest. Yet, every time Imara turned, she could see he kept close behind the frog-boy at a steady trot, his broad bare feet slapping on the mud.

Dikembe walked in front of the other two boys, his head down, keeping his distance from them. The frog-boy was the weakest. As the path climbed steeply upward, he slipped and slithered in the mud. He strained under the sack of plundered rice he was forced to carry. Imara watched the frog-boy stumble many times until he crumpled to his knees, unable to get up. His chest heaved with labored breath.

Rat kicked him. "Get up, Frog! Move!"

Saka dropped his sack to help him up.

"Leave him," snapped Rat. "Frog does this on his own or not at all. We don't waste time on the weak."

Rat stood over the boy as he pulled himself up and hoisted the sack over his back. It was only as they were moving forward again that Imara noticed

Saka had swapped his lighter load for Frog's heavy sack. Rat yelled at Frog again and Imara heard the dull thwack of his rifle butt push Frog forward.

There were only two choices with the Mambas.

Keep up.

Or die.

CHAPTER FOUR

imara

The Black Mamba kept his men at a steady march, following old pathways through the forest, hacking the thick lianas with his panga. He stopped in a clearing, beside a fast stream tumbling over moss-covered rocks. The sun was high overhead and Imara glanced down to see her shadow directly beneath her feet. The hot earth steamed and insects buzzed in the shafts of sunlight.

Imara blinked in the strong light. The Black Mamba's men sank down, dropping their kit bags and guns, some of them falling into sleep as soon as they hit the damp ground.

Imara crouched at the water's edge to splash water over her face. She let it trickle down her neck and soak into her shirt, cooling her skin, washing the sweat and dirt away.

The Black Mamba joined her, filling his bottle from the middle of the stream. "The mountains," he said, pointing to forested mountains reaching up into the clouds. "Soon our search will be over."

The demon whispered in Imara's ear, **Flatter him. Tell him what he wants to hear.**

Imara traced a snake in the dirt beside his feet. "The mountains are your kingdom."

The Black Mamba scooped the dirt-snake and held it in his hand. "My kingdom," he repeated, nodding his head. "This time, I will not let the thieves and traitors take it away from me."

Imara left the Black Mamba staring across to the mountains and made her way upstream, climbing from boulder to boulder. She wanted to be

alone, away from the men. She settled herself on a
damp bed of moss, unlaced her boots and slid her
feet into the water. Her heel was red and raw; the
ragged edges of the blister flapped in the flow of
current. She closed her eyes as the cool water
numbed her skin.

The demon tugged at her consciousness. **He follows you!**

Imara opened her eyes to see Saka squatting on
a stone beside her. He was staring at her feet. She
frowned. How had he slipped away from the
Mamba's guard? How had he come so close without
her hearing him? "What do you want?"

He put his fingers to his lips.

"You can't escape." She nodded to the men lying
farther down the riverbank. "If you try, they will
hunt you down."

Saka shook his head. "I can get something for
your foot. I can make it better."

His voice was low and hushed. He spoke Swahili,
not the Lingala language of the Black Mamba's men.

Don't trust him, Imara, hissed the demon. **He is trying to buy his freedom.**

Imara ran her fingers across the back of her heel. She needed something for the wound. It was red and raw, and getting bigger, making every step painful. She didn't want infection to take hold.

She ignored the demon sniping in her ear and nodded to the boy. "Be quick."

Saka searched along the riverbank, picking clumps of moss-like plants that thrust from between the rocks. He rolled them into a ball and put them in his mouth, chewing them like a goat chewing cud. When green juice began to dribble from the corners of his mouth, he took out the wad of moss and knelt down to press the chewed leaves against her blistered skin. He tore a piece of cotton from his T-shirt to keep the poultice in place.

"It is done," he said. "In three days your foot will be healed."

Imara nodded. She pulled her boot on, careful not to dislodge the dressing and walked back to the clearing followed by Saka. Only Rat was awake as they returned, watching them suspiciously with his small sharp eyes.

Imara ignored him. She was safe. She was the Black Mamba's Spirit Child and no one could touch her. Not even Rat. She pulled some dried meat from her kit bag and chewed it, aware Saka was watching her with hunger in his eyes. His poultice seemed to be helping. The sore no longer burned within her boot. Maybe he could be useful after all. Maybe the small Batwa boy had just bought his freedom.

"Come on! Up! Up!" The Black Mamba kicked his men awake. "We must make it to the base of the mountain by nightfall." He turned to one of his men. "Bundi, how far now?"

Bundi opened a map and spread it on the ground. He pored over it, tracing his finger along the wiggly blue lines of rivers. "Four hours' march, maybe five," he said. Bundi was different from the other men. He was tall and thin, with lighter skin, high cheekbones and a long nose on which perched a pair of glasses. The men distrusted him. He was a man of books. Some said he'd studied in the university in Kinshasa. Some said the Black Mamba had paid him well for his knowledge of the mountains.

Imara hoisted her kit bag on her back and joined the line of men. They were moving slowly now, as the men took turns to hack a new path through the forest. Her feet fell into the steady rhythm of the *ting, ting, ting* of swinging pangas slashing the vines ahead.

All the time they were rising higher, clambering over fallen trees and fording streams. The forest began to change. Here, the trees huddled closer together. The canopy grew thick above, and vines twisted down from the light into the twilight world of the forest floor. These trees were gnarled and squat, hunched over, like fat-bellied old men. Moss covered their twisted branches like wet green fur, glistening with beads of moisture. A steady *pit-pat-*

pit-pat of water dripped from the leaves. Damp fingers of mist reached into Imara's clothes. She shivered and rubbed her bare arms. A fire would be difficult to light tonight.

As the light was fading, Bundi signaled them to stop. He scanned the landscape, tracing the line of a river gulley with his finger. It cut a deep gorge into the mountainside. The water tumbled over small waterfalls and separated into several streams farther down the hillside. The sound of rushing water filled the valley.

Bundi knelt down and pulled at the thick undergrowth to reach the soil beneath. He rubbed the soil between his fingers and looked up at the Black Mamba and nodded.

The Black Mamba clicked his fingers for the three boys to come forward. "Dig," he ordered, pushing a shovel into each of their hands. He aimed his gun at them. "Dig a hole big enough to fit the three of you."

Imara glanced at Black Mamba. He had killed

many, but this was not his way, to make his victims dig their own graves. Dikembe pushed his shovel into the ground, tossing a lump of earth aside, his eyes sliding across to the Black Mamba's gun as he worked. Frog's hands shook as he tried to break up the soft earth and avoid the tree roots. Saka dug hard, shoveling the earth aside, digging deeper and deeper into the ground.

The Mambas sat and watched the boys work until Bundi shone a flashlight into the hole. "It is enough," he said. "Come out now."

The three boys clambered out of the hole, while the Black Mamba walked around its rim, his finger twitching on the trigger of his gun. "Stand aside," he ordered.

Imara turned away. **See!** jeered the demon. **They are to die anyway.**

But it was Bundi who climbed into the hole. Imara could hear him scraping at the soil. He emerged with a pan of muddied stones, which he swirled in the running water of the stream. The Black Mamba

bent down to look. Imara peered over his shoulder, but all she could see were dull gray rocks.

The Black Mamba picked one up and turned it over in his fingers. He looked at Bundi and nodded. A smile broke across his face, his gold tooth glinting in the light from Bundi's flashlight. He held the lump of gray rock up high. "We have found what we came looking for," he said. He reached into a crate for a bottle of banana beer. "Tonight we celebrate."

He bit the metal cap off the beer and spat it on the ground.

"Tomorrow, we dig."

imara

"Coltan!" The Black Mamba took a swig from the bottle. Beer dripped through his smile and trickled down his chin. He kissed the lump of rock and held it high for his men to see. "Columbite-tantalite," he said, rolling the words around his mouth. "Otherwise known as coltan. Needed in every computer and mobile phone in the *world*." He paused and repeated the words slowly for greater effect. "In . . . the . . . *world*! Every country wants it, and we have it here, in Congo. With this rock, we can rule the world. With this rock, we will be rich."

Imara stared at the dull rock. It looked just like any other lump of rock, yet the Black Mamba had trekked miles through the forest and made his men kill for this. She had overheard Bundi say this rock could be worth more than gold.

The men threw their kit bags on the ground outlining their makeshift camp and opened bottles of the stolen beer, flicking the caps into the bush. Rat killed one of the goats, slitting its throat and skinning it, working his knife along the flesh. A cigarette hung from his mouth as he worked, its glowing end bright in the growing darkness. The other goat bleated mournfully from its tether.

As the evening drew in, the air became colder and mist settled in the canopy of leaves above. It was not the fast nightfall of a clear sky, but a slow fading of colors into the night. The Black Mamba tied the three boys together to stop them from escaping into the darkness. Imara watched them shiver and huddle together. Frog curled himself into a ball, his shoulders heaving with silent sobs. Imara noticed Saka grip Frog's hand and hold it in his. Only Dikembe kept his back to the other boys, as if he wanted to separate himself from their weakness.

Imara rubbed her arms and looked around. She felt chill and damp. There was no dry ground to rest on. The forest sagged with the heaviness of water, as if the trees held the rain clouds in their branches. Water glistened on the leaves and swelled the moss and lichens. It hung in veils of fine mist and soaked into the leaf-littered floor. A fire would be difficult to light, but Imara was the Spirit Child. She could do anything. She cleared away the leaves and under-growth to reveal damp earth and unpacked the dry wood, grasses, and charcoal from the bottom of her kit bag. She laid the fire, building up a platform of wood for the grasses and tower of charcoal sticks. She lit the fire with the blue lighter the Black Mamba had given her and gently blew the smoking bundle of grasses until the small flames leaped and took hold.

She would need to cut more wood to cook the

goat meat, and already it was almost too dark to see. She left the men, took her panga and cut her way through the trees, tapping them to see if there were any dead, hollow ones, which would be drier and easier to burn.

She reached a small clearing where the ground had been freshly trampled. Here, branches had been broken, their ragged ends showing the greenwood beneath. Young saplings had been ripped up and tossed aside. A sour musty smell of sweat filled the air. Somewhere beyond the screen of vines, something moved. Something raced past her in the darkness, thumping against the ground.

Imara froze. She felt the hairs on the back of her neck rise. Were there other men in this part of the forest too? Had another rebel group claimed this land? The smell of sweat was pungent now. Imara crouched low and tried to peer through the trees. There was more movement, a crashing in the trees above, and something heavy moving down through the branches, snapping twigs and leaves as it came.

For one brief moment, Imara thought she glimpsed a face watching her from the thick leaf cover, a small black face with amber eyes. But in another moment it was gone. The cracking of undergrowth disappeared into the darkness, leaving only the rasping song of insects and the drip of water from the leaves.

Imara dragged some of the broken branches back to the fire, looking over her shoulder. She shuddered. They were not alone. Maybe there were powerful spirits in this forest, too powerful for her. Maybe they didn't want her here.

That night she feasted with the men on goat meat and bean stew. The goat fat fizzed and flickered in the fire, keeping forest spirits at bay, leaving them dancing in the shadows. The three boys stared hungrily at the food, but Imara knew the Black Mamba didn't feed the new recruits at first. They would have to earn their keep.

As thick mist closed in, the camp fell silent except

for the snores and groans of men, full-bellied and drunk on banana beer. Imara could make out their sleeping forms, huddled under blankets. They slept with their arms around their guns, dreaming of promised riches to come. The Black Mamba slept in a hammock strung between two trees, a tarpaulin tent stretched over him to keep him dry.

The three boys were quiet now too. These boys were young, too young. The Black Mamba should have killed them or let them escape into the forest. Ones like these were no use to anyone. Imara had heard Frog moaning and whimpering as the daylight faded. He had called for his mama, like the new recruits always did at first. But she had covered her ears, knowing that the ones who cried loudest for their mothers were always the first to die.

Imara wrapped herself in her blanket and the sheet of plastic she kept bundled in her kit bag. Her skin prickled with cold. She was colder than she had ever been before. She shuffled closer to the fire for warmth. A restless wind swirled the smoke low across the ground and the embers crawled with worms of light. She lay down and tried to sleep, but sleep wouldn't find her. She turned her face away from the firelight, glad of the darkness. It hid the scar and let the devil inside her sleep. The darkness was a place where secrets could escape into the night and silent tears flow.

"Imara?"

Imara held her breath. The Black Mamba was awake. She could hear his footsteps on the damp ground. She sat up, keeping her face in the shadows as he crouched next to her. He seemed even bigger in the darkness, filling up the night-space between them. She didn't look at him, but fixed her eyes on the snake-bone amulet around his wrist.

"Spirit Child . . . ," he whispered.

Imara felt the demon stir inside her at the sound of his voice. She poked at the fire with a long stick, sending sparks up into the air.

"I need to ask something of you," said the Black

Mamba. He twirled the snake bones. "Are we safe here?"

Imara could see his hand shaking as he touched the amulet, his lips moving as he silently counted the snake bones. She had never seen the Black Mamba fear anything before. Maybe the Black Mamba let his secrets slip out into the darkness too.

He needs you for his protection, the demon whispered in her ear. **And that gives us power.**

"Imara!" The Black Mamba's face was so close she could smell the stale tobacco on his breath. He gripped her arm, his fingers digging into her skin. "Are we safe here? Will the spirits protect us?"

Tell him, Imara! Tell him what we saw today!

"Imara! I need to know."

Tell him, Imara. . . . Tell him what we saw in the forest.

Imara pulled her arm away from the Black Mamba's grip. The image of the small face behind the forest vines filled her mind. She stirred the fire, so that more sparks spiraled upward.

"We are safe," said Imara. She paused. "For now, at least."

The Black Mamba stared into the flames. "What is it that you see?"

Imara traced a face in the hot ashes of the fire. "The forest has eyes," she whispered. "We are being watched."

bobo

Bobo pulled his blanket over his head. He closed his eyes, but sleep wouldn't find him. He could hear the steady breathing of his sister on the mattress beside him and the rain drumming on the corrugated iron roof above. The clouds on the mountains had descended on the town. Outside, a few cars swished through the wide puddles, their headlights briefly lighting up the room.

Bobo turned onto his back. The rain usually soothed him, but tonight was different. Tonight, something was wrong.

The light from the paraffin lamp flickered from the next room. He could hear his baby brother's cry and his mother's soothing words.

Bobo swung his legs out of bed and followed the soft lamplight into the next room.

"Is Papa home yet?" he asked.

His mother shook her head, rocking the baby in the shawl tied around her chest. The baby closed his eyes, one small brown hand outstretched in sleep.

"It is late," said Bobo. He crossed the room and opened the door onto the night. Water pooled into the room and a moth batted past him, finding the light.

"Tsk! Bobo, do not let the night in," scolded his mother.

"There was gunfire in the mountains today," said Bobo. "Mbeze says the rebels are back."

"Mbeze says many things," said Mama. "He likes to drink and tell big stories."

"But Papa was in the mountains today, and he is not yet home."

Mama picked up her needle and began sewing thread into the soft green beret on the table. "Papa is on duty with Kambale, the head ranger today. Kambale knows the mountains better than anyone. Papa will be safe."

"No one is safe from the bullets," said Bobo.

Mama dimmed the lamp. "Papa will be fine. He said he was tracking the Tumaini gorilla group to see if Heri has given birth." She smiled, stroking the baby's soft head. "It could happen any time in the next few weeks. Every birth is important for the gorillas. You know that. Papa said he might be late tonight."

Bobo sat down at the table and ran his fingers across the green beret, letting them linger on the gorilla badge.

"See?" Mama smiled, showing Bobo Papa's name embroidered inside the beret's rim. "Look at Papa's new beret. We must be proud that he is being made a senior ranger of the park."

"I'll stay up and wait for him," said Bobo.

Mama shook her head. "Tsk! Go to bed, Bobo.

You have school tomorrow. Staying awake will not bring him back to us any faster."

Bobo climbed back into bed. He was falling asleep when he heard running feet splashing through the puddles and the stomp, stomp, stomp of boots on the porch. He crept out of bed and stood in the shadows by the door and watched Papa step into the house, his green cape dripping water on the floor. Mama wrapped her arms around her husband, held him tight, and would not let go.

"I was worried," she whispered. "There has been talk of rebels in the mountains."

Bobo held his breath, straining his ears to hear them talk.

Papa stroked the head of the baby cradled in the shawl. "Mbeze is right for once. There have been killings on the other side of the mountains. Rebels have crossed from the lowland sector of the park. These are new rebels, a different group. Some call them the Black Mambas."

Mama shivered. "I have heard of them. They say

the Mambas have a Spirit Child who speaks the devil's tongue and gives them power. Mbeze said if you kill one man, two more rise up to fight."

"Pah!" Papa shook his head. "Men die only once."

"Did you see them?"

Papa nodded. "They didn't see us."

"Are there many?"

"About twenty-five, maybe thirty." He took a deep breath and pulled Mama and the baby closer. "They have kadogo too."

Mama sucked air sharply through her teeth. "Ay ay ay!"

"We are safe in town," said Papa. "But keep the children close to home."

Bobo felt his heart thump inside his chest. Kadogo! Child soldiers. Killers. They feared nothing and followed their leaders to the death.

Mama shook her head. "There haven't been rebels in this part of the park for a long while now. What are they doing here?"

"Maybe they are passing through the mountains," reassured Papa. "Kambale has asked me to return with him tomorrow and move the Tumaini group away from them, toward this side of the mountain."

Mama cradled the baby close to her. "And what if they see you this time? What will you do?"

Bobo stepped out into the light. He picked up the house broom from behind the door and held the broom like a gun, firing imaginary bullets into the room. "*Ak . . . ak . . . ak . . . ak . . . ak!* I will come with you and shoot them dead."

"Bobo!" Papa snatched the broom from him. "If you want to be a wildlife ranger, use your head, not a gun. Rangers use guns for defense only."

Bobo tried to snatch back the broom. "Why not kill them? Shoot them first before they shoot you."

Papa held the broom high out of reach. "Only a weak man needs a gun to make him strong, Bobo. These men are cowards. Do you want to be like them too?"

Bobo clenched and unclenched his fists. "They

have no right in the mountains. What if they are here to kill the gorillas, what then?"

"That is why I must move the Tumaini group away from the rebels. We need to keep them safe."

Bobo shoved his hands deep in the pockets of his shorts and paced up and down the room. "What about Heri? Has she given birth yet?"

Papa smiled. "Not yet. It could be tomorrow, it could be next month. It is hard to say. But she is well, and that's what matters. Come," he said, pulling a camera out from his rucksack. "Let me show you the photos I took today."

Bobo sat down next to Papa at the table and held the camera, scrolling through the images on the screen. He loved looking at the photos his father took for the researchers while he tracked the gorillas.

Papa pointed to an image of a large gorilla with his fists against his chest. "Hodari was not pleased to see us today. I think he was unsettled by the rebels in the forest."

Bobo stared at Hodari, the huge silverback

gorilla, and the leader of the Tumaini group. Bobo had seen him in the forest on a trip with Papa. He remembered feeling dwarfed by the size of him, his huge domed head and powerful back and shoulders covered in fine silvery fur. He remembered the smell of him, a musty, sour odor that reached through the forest. Yet, despite their size, Papa always said gorillas were the gentlest of creatures. They would only ever attack if members of their family were threatened.

"And here is Heri," said Papa, flicking to the next image. "She is keeping herself away from the others. See, Hisani, the oldest female, is interested in her. I think she is checking she is okay."

"And where is Hisani's son?" said Bobo, keen to see his favorite gorilla.

Papa laughed. "Wait till you see. He is nearly eighteen months and getting more daring every day." He flicked to the next image of a young gorilla holding a notebook, trying to rip the pages from it. "He loves my notebook and tries to eat it. He thinks the pages are strange flat white leaves he can chew. Today Enzi, the young blackback, chased him round and round and round to try to get the notebook for himself."

Bobo smiled at the young blackback trying hard to be like the mature silverback, but unable to resist playing chasing games with the younger gorilla too. "Is there a name for Hisani's son?" said Bobo.

"Not yet. Kambale is trying to see if we can find someone to sponsor him and give him a name. It could bring much-needed money to the park."

Bobo flicked through all the images of the day. His face became serious. "There is one missing."

Papa frowned. "No, there can't be. I took a photo of each gorilla of the Tumaini group." He held out his hand for the camera. "Let me see."

A smile twitched on Bobo's mouth. "There is definitely one member of the group missing. The ugly one!" He lifted the camera to his eye and pointed it at his father. "Smile, Papa!"

"Be careful with that camera," Papa said sharply.

"It belongs to the national park authorities, not to us."

Mama laughed. She pushed the green beret toward him. "Tsk! Put this on and let Bobo take a picture of his father."

Papa relented and pulled the new beret onto his head.

"Smile, gorilla-man," said Bobo.

Papa's face broke into a wide, wide smile.

Bobo clicked the shutter. "Done."

Papa reached across and put the beret on Bobo's head and pulled it down over his eyes. "One day, you might be wearing one of these too."

"Then let me come with you tomorrow," begged Bobo. "You promised me I could come with you again one day."

"No, Bobo."

"Please!"

Papa shook his head and lifted the cloth from the bowl of food Mama had saved for him. He looked tired and weary, too tired to argue. "Bobo, it is time for you to go to bed. You have school tomorrow.

One day you can come with me, but now is not the time. It is not safe at the moment."

"I'm not scared, Papa. I am fourteen already. I don't need school. I am old enough to carry a gun into the forest."

Papa sat back in his chair and looked Bobo in the eyes. "Boboto, my son. The gun has caused too many deaths, too much sadness in this country. Go to school before you become a ranger. It is books and learning that will make you strong."

gorilla

Hisani's son pulled more leaves around him and pushed his fingers into the fur of his mother's back. He could hear her soft breathing and feel the steady rise and fall of her chest. He closed his eyes, but sleep would not come. The night's quickness was replaced by a long dark waking, filled with racing images of the Tall Apes in the forest.

These were new Tall Apes. They were not the harmless Watchers who kept their vigil on the gorilla family. They were not the Hunters who moved silently through the forest with their dogs. These new Tall Apes were not of the forest. The thunder from their fire-sticks had silenced the *birds and sent the animals deep into the undergrowth.*

They had arrived, bringing their noise and sweat with them. Hisani's son had stayed close to his mother, hidden in the thick leaves. He had watched the new Tall Apes pass, their feet sliding and slipping on the mud, their fire-sticks swinging on their backs. The young gorilla hadn't seen so many Tall Apes before, but this group wasn't a family group. It was a big troop, a male group, of adults and young. There was one female too, but she showed no bond to the other Tall Apes. She kept her head down and distanced herself from the others. They had passed almost close enough to touch, but his mother had held him, and wrapped her great arm around him, willing him to be silent and still.

Hodari, the silverback, was wary of these new Tall Apes. His fear odor, pungent in the damp air, had sent a warning to the other gorillas. Even with his strength and back of silvery fur, he didn't confront the new Tall Apes. He didn't mock-charge them like he did to the Watchers when they ventured too close. He sensed a greater danger. Instead, he had moved his family higher up the mountain, where he settled them for the night, pulling leaves and branches around himself, a sign they should do the same.

But the female Tall Ape had come close again, swinging a cutting stick through the forest, bringing down the vines and small branches. Hodari had woken his family and moved them on again in the darkness. But Hisani's son had stopped for a moment, hidden in the vines as his family moved away. He had wanted a closer look at these strange apes. This female Tall Ape looked wary, casting her eyes around. She stood still, listening to the sounds of the retreating gorillas, keeping low to the ground, her muscles tensed and ready to run, like she was prey.

Hisani's son moved a little closer, pushing vines aside to get a better view. For a moment the Tall Ape's face appeared close to his. Her smooth brown face was scarred like the fighting face of a silverback that had seen many battles. For a brief moment, her eyes met his, and they stared, each one taking in the other. Then Hisani's son pulled away, scrambling through the undergrowth, hooting for his mother. He climbed on her back and clung to her as they followed Hodari to higher ground.

As he curled up with his mother in their new nest of leaves high in the branches, he could hear Hodari stirring on the ground below. Not even the great silverback could find sleep tonight. Maybe the images of the new Tall Apes unsettled him too.

Hisani's son closed his eyes and saw the face of the female Tall Ape in his mind, bright in the darkness. It stared right at him.

Right into him.

His fur prickled with fear.

He had put his family at risk.

He had let himself be seen.

CHAPTER SEVEN

bobo

Bobo knew the snake was somewhere in the undergrowth. He could hear the rattle of dried seed heads as it wound its way between the brittle grasses. He caught glimpses of the curves of its body, of its rippling dark-gray scales.

A black mamba.

The deadliest snake in Africa.

Its defense was its attack.

Death's shadow was sliding toward him.

Bobo couldn't move. He couldn't run. He couldn't scream.

He stared, transfixed as the snake flowed toward him. It rose up in front of Bobo.

Up

and up

and up,

until its coffin-shaped head was level with his. Its tongue flickered, tasting Bobo, tasting his breath. Bobo stared into the small black eyes.

Time slowed down.

The world stopped turning.

Bobo watched as the black mamba lunged forward, opening its wide black mouth.

Fangs glistened with droplets of venom.

Death was coming.

Bobo sat up, sucking air deep into his chest. His heart hammered and he gripped the edges of his bed, trying to pull himself out of sleep, out of the nightmare.

A blue dawn light lifted the darkness from the room. He could make out the usual shapes inside: his sister curled up on the mattress next to him, the cotton curtains, and the cupboard, his school bag slung across the chair.

Everything looked the same but he felt different inside.

The tight knot of worry from the night before stayed with him.

The smell of coffee sifted into the room and he could hear Mama patting cassava dough on the table.

Bobo swung his legs off the bed, pulled on his T-shirt and shorts, and went to find his mother.

He looked around the room. "Where is Papa?"

Mama looked up from her kneading. "He left early. Kambale's wife called round late last night to say Kambale is sick, so April, the receptionist, is giving Papa a lift to work instead."

"He's gone already?"

Mama nodded. "Just now. April is picking him up from the end of the road."

"You should have woken me." In two leaps Bobo was at the front door. "I have to see him."

"Bobo!" called Mama.

But Bobo was already running, his bare feet slapping on the cracked tarmac, flying down the street toward his father.

"Papa! . . . Papa!"

Bobo saw his father standing at the end of the street beside the market. The sun had not yet risen, yet the stallholders were arriving in the pre-dawn light, setting up their stalls. Steel drums were burning charcoal, the embers glowing red hot, ready to cook hot snacks of plantain fritters and grilled corn. Bobo's father stood on the street corner, stamping his feet in the cool morning. His new green beret sat at an angle on his head, and he was wearing the cape and rubber boots he would need in the mountains.

"Papa! . . . Papa!"

Papa turned toward him. "Bobo, what are you doing here?"

"Don't go, Papa. I had a dream. A black mamba . . . maybe it is a warning."

Papa put his hand on Bobo's shoulder. "A dream is just a dream, nothing more."

60

"Well let me come with you then."

"Bobo, I have already told you that one day I will take you with me, but not today."

"But you will need me," pleaded Bobo. "Mama said Kambale is sick. You can't go into the mountains alone."

"I will be fine. The Tumaini group knows me better than anyone. It will draw too much attention if many rangers go in. Bobo, I know these forests. These rebels are clumsy." Papa smiled. "They will not see me. You know me. I can move as silently as a leopard."

Bobo shook his head. "Francois was killed by rebels last year. He knew the forests too."

Papa sighed. "I know. Francois was a brave man, but there were many rebels that day. Francois was confronting them over illegal charcoal burning. All I am going to do is to move the gorillas to this side of the mountain. I have no intention of coming into contact with the rebels."

"Will you be back tonight?"

Papa shrugged his shoulders. "It depends. I may be several days if the Tumaini group are slow to move."

Bobo held on to his father's arm. "What about the black mamba? What about my dream? I don't want to lose you."

"Bobo." Papa smiled. "I am your father. Nothing can change that."

Bobo felt a pit in his stomach. He thought of the Black Mamba and the Spirit Child. These were new rebels. Powerful. They had dark magic on their side. "They have a Spirit Child, Papa. She can put a curse on you."

Papa shook his head. "The rebels' greatest weapon is fear, and I choose not to be afraid."

"Don't go, not this time. I have a bad feeling about today."

"Boboto, my son. I have to go. Look, there is April waiting for me."

A car horn beeped and Bobo could see the receptionist drumming her fingers on the steering wheel.

"Why? Why you?" Bobo clung to his father, furious with the hot tears that ran down his face. He felt more like seven years old than fourteen.

Bobo's father put his arm around him. "Do you remember me telling you why I must do this? Do you remember what I told you, when we sat and watched the dawn together in the mountains?"

Bobo frowned and wiped the tears away with his hand. "That was a long time ago."

Papa smiled. "Then let me tell you again."

"Papa! I don't want a lecture. I don't want you to go."

"Listen," said Papa. "I tell you this because it is important that you know. It is important that you know your father." He pointed to the rim of golden light brimming above the horizon. "Bobo, my son, what do you see?"

Bobo stared hard, remembering his father's words from before, knowing them by heart. He clung to his father. "Papa . . . I see the sun rise."

"Now close your eyes and tell me what you *feel*."

Bobo closed his eyes. "I feel the whole world turning beneath my feet."

Papa pulled his son to him. "And as it turns, we turn with it. You and me . . . we are all part of it. Everything we are, everything we do connects us with it. Breathe this air. Drink this rain. The earth pulses with the life it gives us. But if we lose our love of it, then we lose everything. But most of all, we lose ourselves. We lose our souls. So, Bobo, what gives me the right to sit back and do nothing to protect it? With every dawn, I must ask myself: Who am I? What is my part in this? How am I going to use *this* day, to make tomorrow a better world?"

The car horn sounded a second time.

Papa held Bobo's face in his hands and looked into his eyes. "Do you understand why I must go?"

Bobo nodded and closed his eyes, trying to stop the tears from falling.

"You see," said Papa. "I have no choice."

CHAPTER EIGHT

bobo

The horn beeped again and Bobo's father gave him a quick hug and hurried to the waiting car, waving once before he shut the door. Bobo watched until the car's red taillights disappeared into the line of traffic.

"Hey, Bobo!"

Bobo turned around. Lamu was walking toward him, his school bag slung across his shoulder, kicking a ball along the ground.

Bobo wiped his tears, hoping Lamu wouldn't see.

Lamu scooped up the ball and bounced it to

Bobo. "What do you think of this one?"

Bobo caught the ball and turned it over in his hands. It was one of Lamu's home-styled soccer balls, made from plastic bags and tied with string. "What's so different about it?"

"This is an improved design." Lamu grinned. "Old bicycle inner tubes for extra bounce."

Bobo bounced it on the ground. "Cool," he said. He dribbled it forward, in and out of people walking along the street.

"Hey," called Lamu. "Give it back."

"Come and get it," yelled Bobo.

Bobo sprinted along the road, kicking the ball ahead of him. He could hear Lamu close behind, his flip-flops slapping on the ground. Bobo knew he wouldn't be able to keep it. Lamu was the best soccer player in school. Lamu whacked his bag against Bobo, knocking him aside.

"Foul!" yelled Bobo. "Red card."

But Lamu tackled the ball from him and gave it a kick, sending it flying into a pile of bins. "Goal!"

yelled Lamu as the bins reeled and clattered into the road.

Bobo laughed. "Come on, walk with me to school. I have to go home and get changed and pick up my bag first."

"Tsk," Mama tutted, seeing Bobo walk in the house with his feet covered in dust and mud. She offered Lamu some water while Bobo washed and put on the pale blue shirt and black shorts of his school uniform.

"How is your father, Lamu?" asked Mama. "I am sorry to hear Kambale isn't well enough to join Bobo's father today."

"He's a little better this morning, thank you," said Lamu. "The doctor thinks it may be malaria again."

Mama handed Bobo cassava bread wrapped in a clean cloth as he headed out the door. "Bobo," she called after him. "Don't forget to take your sister to school!"

"She'd better hurry," said Bobo, waiting by the door. "Or she'll have to walk to school alone."

Mama shook her head. "You heard what Papa said about the rebels. You must walk her to school. All the way, understand? You must walk her right to the front door. Promise me?"

Bobo glanced at Lamu. "I promise, Mama."

Mama nodded. "And do not go talking to any strangers in town today."

Bobo rolled his eyes. "Yes, Mama."

"Bobo, this is not a game," she said sharply. "If anyone tries to stop you, you take her hand and run."

Bobo's sister opened the door. "Who is going to stop us?"

"No one," said Mama. "Come on, all of you. It is time you left for school."

Bobo walked with his sister and Lamu to school. The sun had risen above the rooftops, into a pale yellow sky. The buildings cast long zebra-striped shadows and dust sparkled in a haze above the road. The air was thick and humid, yet far away on the horizon, clouds were forming over the mountains.

Bobo watched his sister skip ahead. "Have you heard about the rebels?"

Lamu lowered his voice and nodded. "The Black Mamba is in the mountains."

Bobo glanced at Lamu. "Mbeze says they have a Spirit Child. If you look into her eyes you see your death."

"My father saw the snake sign carved into a tree in the forest." Lamu lowered his voice even more. "They say it is a curse. I think that is why he is sick today."

"You said he had malaria."

Lamu shrugged his shoulders. "They use the darkest form of magic."

"They will be gone soon," said Bobo. "Papa says they are passing through."

Lamu shook his head. "My father says they have carved snake signs on many trees on the other side of the mountain. He thinks they are here to stay."

"Have they come for the gorillas?"

Lamu shook his head. "They come for what

everyone comes for . . . the gold and tin, but mostly they come for the coltan."

Bobo shuddered. He had heard of the coltan mines in the lowland sector of the park, mines ruled by armed gangs and rebels. It was too dangerous for the rangers to patrol that area. The mines destroyed the forest. They cut deep into the earth, the trees torn down for charcoal and the wildlife killed for bush-meat. Papa had said that many gorillas had been wiped out and only a handful of forest elephants had survived the years of war. Maybe the highland sector would become too dangerous to visit too. Bobo knew the rangers wanted the tourists back to see the gorillas and bring money to the park. "The gorillas will suffer," said Bobo.

Lamu threw his ball at Bobo's chest. "Gorillas! Is that all you think about?"

Bobo threw it back. "You're not going to be a ranger, like your father?"

Lamu laughed. "Can't you tell you are looking at the greatest soccer player of all time? I can't waste my talents. I'm going to play for the Congo in the World Cup."

Bobo broke into a smile. He kicked the ball and watched Lamu as he charged after it.

"Come on," yelled Lamu. "Race you to school."

"Coming!" shouted Bobo.

Bobo dropped his sister off at her school, and watched her take her teacher's hand and follow her into the class.

He turned for one last look at the mountains.

In the distance, massing clouds unfurled across the sky, their dark-gray underbellies folding over the forest, obscuring it from view. The rumble of thunder rolled across the valley. Bobo thought of the gorillas and rebels on the far side of the mountain. He thought of Papa trekking toward them.

His father was heading right into a storm.

CHAPTER NINE

imara

*I*mara stirred and scratched at the fresh insect bites she had gained in the night. The thick sweet scent of ripe mangos hung in the air around her. She opened one eye and watched the woman with the coffee-colored skin kneeling beside her. The woman was smiling and humming softly. The tune had floated through Imara's dream, familiar, yet drifting somewhere just beyond her memory. Imara tried to stay in sleep, but she could feel the demon rising deep inside. She reached out her hand, but the woman dissolved into the light, slipping between the worlds of wake and sleep, the sweet scent of mangos fading with her.

Imara sat up and rubbed her eyes. She was cold and wet. The night's rain had crept into the plastic sheet she had wrapped around herself and her muscles were tight and stiff from sleeping on the damp earth. The bitter smell of smoke clung to her blanket and her skin. She breathed out, watching her breath rise in spirals of mist in the cool air.

Above, beyond the framework of leaves and branches, light was coming back into the sky. The darkness of the night was softening. Imara could make out the shapes of the men wrapped in blankets. Even Rat was slumped forward, his gun fallen out of his arms onto the damp ground. It wouldn't be long before the morning light filtered to the forest floor. But Imara knew she had plenty of time today. The men would sleep long into the morning, full on fresh meat and beer.

Imara allowed herself a smile. This was her time. When the men were deep in sleep the devil inside her slumbered too. She sat up and shook out her blanket, shaking out the dirt and bugs from the night. She was still cold and the day promised more rain. Above, the clouds glowed with the deep blue light of a coming storm. She rubbed her arms and pushed the log in the fire with her foot. The fire was awake despite the night rain, the glow of embers still crawling in the ash beneath blackened half-burned wood. She pulled dry grasses from her kit bag and blew softly, letting the flames catch. The smoke curled and trailed across the forest floor. The air was idle and sleepy, like the men. She placed the last supply of charcoal on the fire. They would need more charcoal soon.

She moved closer to the fire for warmth and removed her boot, examining her raw heel. The poultice had helped, although it had turned slimy and slipped from her foot.

"Let me make another poultice for you." Imara looked up to see Saka watching her.

The demon inside Imara snapped awake. **Don't**

trust him. He wants our fire. He wants our heat.

"You need more moss to make it better," he said. "I will find it for you in the stream we passed not far from here."

Don't trust him.

Imara glanced at the Black Mamba lying in his hammock. She could see his chest rising and falling as he slept. Maybe Saka could find more of the plants for her foot before the men woke up. She needed something. She'd seen grown men lose their feet from gangrene, where sores had turned into infected wounds.

Imara watched Saka. Frog was awake beside him too, although Dikembe slumbered, his eyes twitching beneath their lids.

Imara rose, holding her gun close to her. She reached down to untie Saka and Frog, then stood back and aimed the gun at them both as they rubbed their wrists. She kicked an empty water can toward Frog. "Get up," she ordered in a harsh whisper. "Both of you. Come and fetch water and firewood."

Saka pulled Frog to his feet and whispered words Imara couldn't hear. "No talking," snapped Imara. "Move."

She walked behind them, following Saka as he led them to the end of the river gorge where the fast water separated into small streams rushing down through rocky gullies. Saka crouched down and started foraging for moss along the riverbank.

Imara nodded at Frog. "Fill the can from the fast water in the middle of the stream," she ordered.

The boy waded in, leaning against the fast flow of the current and filled his can. He stumbled back to join her on the bank, spilling some water. Imara could see his hands shaking and his cheeks were wet with tears. The demon writhed inside, clawing and pulling at her.

Don't let him in, Imara. He is weak. He will destroy you if you let him in.

Imara jabbed Frog with her rifle butt. "Don't cry!" she yelled.

The boy squeezed his eyes tight but his breath

caught in his throat. He bent over, his chest heaving with silent sobs.

Imara kicked him. "Don't cry. Keep your tears inside. Your mama is not here for you now." She walked away, leaving him curled on the ground, his arms wrapped around his stomach.

Well done, Imara. Well done.

Imara turned and spat onto the ground. "Bring a full can of water, or don't come back at all." She pulled her panga and began to hack at young saplings to take back for the fire, wiping the sweat from her forehead. The day was heating up, the clouds building higher in the sky. Wispy tendrils of mist reached down and trailed across the treetops. In the river, Saka was helping Frog fill the water can. Imara could see him whispering to Frog.

"No talking!" she shouted. "Where is my poultice?"

"I have it," called Saka. He scrambled out of the water and laid the wad of chewed moss on a flat stone on the riverbank.

Imara pushed her hand into the small of her back and leaned her panga beside the cut saplings. She slung her rifle across her shoulders and slid down the rocks to join him, removing her boot to wash her heel in the flowing water. She rested her foot on the rock to dry, and closed her eyes, listening to the heavy silence of the forest. The mist was pressing in, muffling the sounds of the rush of the river. Even the drone of insects seemed dulled in the thick air. At least the men wouldn't be marching today. If the Black Mamba decided to set up camp here then it would give her time to rest her foot. Imara tore a strip of the bottom of her shirt and tied the poultice in place, pulling her boot on. Maybe she should get Saka to pick some more moss for a poultice for the next day too.

"Saka!" she called.

She turned, but the boy had disappeared. All she could see was Frog standing beside the cut saplings, his eyes wide.

Imara jumped to her feet and lifted her rifle to

her shoulder. "Where is Saka?" she demanded.

Frog just stared into the forest.

Imara stared after him, into the dark spaces between the trees.

But there was no one there.

The small Batwa boy and Imara's panga were gone.

Saka was nowhere to be seen.

imara

You stupid girl! screamed the demon. **I told you not to trust the boy. If the Black Mamba sees your weakness, you know what he will do to you!**

"Where is he?" yelled Imara, aiming her rifle at Frog's chest.

Frog just stared at Imara, his eyes bulging, the water can shaking in his hand.

"MOVE!" yelled Imara, jabbing her rifle in the direction of the camp. "Or I shoot."

Imara forced Frog at a steady march back to

camp. Thunder rumbled in the sky above as the clouds swelled with more rain. The forest floor darkened, even though it was not yet midday.

When Imara reached the camp, the Black Mamba and the men were already awake. The Black Mamba was strutting with his hands behind his back, barking orders at his men.

Imara pushed the end of one of the saplings into the fire and hung the water over the flames to boil. "We need more charcoal. This forest wood is too wet to burn."

The Black Mamba pointed to a stack of cut wood the men were covering with earth. "Soon we will have as much charcoal as we need."

Imara looked across at the charcoal kiln the men were making. From the size of it, it was clear the Black Mamba was in no hurry to leave this place.

The Black Mamba glanced around. "Where is the Batwa boy?" he grunted.

Imara tried to keep her hands steady as she poured water into the pan of mealie maize. The demon turned somersaults inside. "He is gone," she said.

The Black Mamba's eyes widened. "Gone? Escaped?"

Imara nodded and stirred the porridge, chasing the spoon round and round the side of the pot.

Slow down . . . hissed the demon. **Don't let him see your fear.**

The Black Mamba shook his head. "But you said to let him live, Imara."

Rat narrowed his eyes. "Maybe Imara was wrong this time? Maybe her powers are weakening."

Imara took a deep breath. "I have cursed the boy," she said. "If he does not return by nightfall, he will die in the forest."

The Black Mamba kicked the fire. "I hope for his sake he dies in the forest. It will be better than what I will do to him if he returns."

Imara kept out of the Black Mamba's way all day. She made herself a shelter of leaves and branches and watched the men clear a patch of level ground beyond the river gorge. She listened to the steady thwack of axes. Huge trees groaned and fell, opening up the sky. Bundi ordered the men to dig up stumps and roots. He wanted the area to be flat and level. He paced around it, looking up to the sky. The Black Mamba joined him, nodding in approval. She heard them talking about a blue bird flying in from the east, but when she looked, all she could see were the dark gray clouds and the coming rain.

Dikembe and Frog were kept busy cutting and stacking wood, building another kiln to burn wood to make charcoal. They heaped leaves and damp soil onto the wood and stood back when the kiln was lit, the burning wood sending blue smoke up into the air. Soon there would be plenty of fuel, but the food was running low. Imara counted three sacks of rice stolen from the village. There would be enough for another week, maybe. But to feed thirty men, they would need more soon. The men would want meat too, and that would mean another raid. She wondered how far the nearest villages were from here.

Rain had fallen steadily all through the afternoon, dripping through the trees, scouring the loose soil. The water ran bloodred across the ground.

Imara wrapped her plastic sheet around her, and worked hard to keep the fire alight. She didn't want to anger the Black Mamba again today. The fire smoked with the damp wood, but burned just hot enough to boil rice for the men. Rat slaughtered the last goat, the last of the fresh meat in camp, and cut it into chunks to cook in the pot too.

As night closed in, the men left their work clearing the trees and gathered around the fire for food and warmth. The Black Mamba slung the finished rice pan to Dikembe and Frog. "Share what's left between you."

Dikembe snatched it and turned his back on Frog, crouching over the pan like a dog over a bone. Imara watched him wipe his fingers around the base to scrape the last few grains of rice, glancing back at Frog with quick sharp eyes, daring him to challenge him. Hunger changed people. Dikembe was beginning to understand the laws of the forest. Only the strong survive.

Imara cradled her own cup of rice and slunk back into the shadows, scraping the rice out and sucking the starchy water from her fingers.

As the daylight faded, a figure emerged from the shadows of the forest.

Rat shot to his feet, pointing his gun at the incomer. "Who's there?"

Saka walked into the firelight, an antelope slung across his back and a large chickenlike bird hanging from a twisted vine in his hand. Imara could see her own panga dangling from his waist.

The Black Mamba circled the boy. He pushed the end of his panga into his chest. "No one runs from the Black Mamba and lives," he said.

Saka dropped the antelope at the Black Mamba's feet, the limp body thudding on the ground. He held up the bird. "I have found bush-meat for you."

"I say kill him," said Rat.

Imara watched the Black Mamba from the

85

shadows. He stroked the stubble on his chin.

"He's a spy," whispered Rat.

Saka held the dead bird even higher. "You need meat and I can find more. Much more. I can track anything: antelope, bush-pig, monkey, porcupine. I can find gorilla, too."

"Gorilla?" said the Black Mamba. He let his panga drop away from Saka's chest. "Gorilla? Are you sure?"

The boy nodded.

"Tell me," the Black Mamba said. "Are there gorilla here?"

Saka nodded again. "Very close."

"Are there young ones? Babies?"

"Yes," said Saka, pointing into the forest. "I've seen them, not far from here."

The Black Mamba smiled, showing his gold tooth. His eyes searched out Imara in the shadows. "Well," he said, "it seems our Spirit Child was right to let the Batwa boy live. He will be very useful to us, after all."

CHAPTER ELEVEN

imara

In just five days, Imara had watched the Black Mamba's men clear the lower slopes around the river gorge. The Mambas dug into the rich soil and opened up the ground like a wound, the red soil exposed like flesh. The men worked with spades and trowels, their bodies covered in mud as they hauled out the dull gray rocks of coltan to be washed and sifted.

The news of the Black Mamba's coltan mine spread like wind across the forest, reaching the villages and the refugee camps where people lived, displaced by war. Men came at first. Thin men, with broken teeth and broken lives. Then women and children started arriving from their villages, all coming to find fortune in the mine.

Bundi set up a trading post beneath a sheet of tarpaulin where he put himself in charge of taking names. He pushed his glasses on his nose and took details of all new miners in a creased and dog-eared ledger. The line of people wanting to work in the mine became longer each day. Imara sat down beside him and handed out the toughened sacks for the coltan.

"Next," called Bundi.

A young man stepped forward, shovel in hand.

"Name," said Bundi.

"Frederick," said the man. "Frederick Ntanga."

Imara watched Bundi write, the mysterious loops and swirls of words appearing like magic on the page.

Bundi looked up. "You are here to work in the mines?"

Frederick nodded.

"Do you have a permit?" said Bundi.

"A permit?"

"You must pay the Black Mamba a hundred-dollar payment to work in the mine. Do you have that money?"

Frederick shook his head.

Bundi tapped his pen on the desk. "There is another payment for food, water, and firewood."

"I have no money," said Frederick.

Imara glanced at him. He was like the rest. No one had any money.

Bundi looked at Frederick over the top of his glasses. "You can start work, but you must pay back the Black Mamba before you can keep any money yourself," he said. "Work hard and you will pay it back quickly. Do you understand?"

The man nodded.

"Then sign here," said Bundi. "If you can't write, then sign an X, like this."

The man gripped the pen and signed an X by his

name on the ledger. Imara handed him a sack and watched him head toward the mine. She had heard Bundi tell the Black Mamba it would be months before any of the workers would earn any real pay at all.

Imara was free to walk among the miners. None dared look at her. They fell silent and kept their eyes down to the ground as she passed. The tales about her had spread far and wide. She was the Black Mamba's Spirit Child. She could curse your soul. To look into her eyes was to see your death.

Only the Black Mamba and Saka looked in her eyes. Maybe Saka had already faced his death before. Each day he disappeared into the forest and each evening he brought back more bush-meat, laying it at the Black Mamba's feet for him to have first choice. Every evening Imara watched Saka lie down next to Frog to sleep, their backs touching. In the day they moved around each other, careful not to show eye contact, careful not to let people hear them talk. Only Imara saw their silent friendship, an invisible bond between them. Only she saw the food parcels wrapped in leaves that Saka dropped at Frog's feet. No one else saw the boys' friendship, only Imara. Friendship was forbidden in camp. It was a dangerous secret to have. Imara smiled inwardly. To know someone's secret was to hold them in your power.

The camp fell into a daily routine, something life with the Mambas hadn't offered before. The Black Mamba had sent Frog to work in the mine, and Dikembe to train to be a soldier. Imara watched Dikembe's face harden as Rat put him through his paces, doing squat-jumps, press-ups, firing practice, and runs with full packs into the forest. He was rewarded with food and beer, and he made sure he kept himself away from Saka and Frog.

Imara watched them all from the shadows. The demon kept her company while she tended the fire, cooked meals for the men, and washed their clothes. At night, she wrapped herself in her sleeping mat, preferring to now sleep in the crook of the tree, rather than the damp forest floor where she was often woken by charging lines of army ants. Her stomach churned with hunger. Except for the bush-meat Saka brought in, there was no more food to feed the growing hoard of miners. The Mambas would have to raid another village soon. She could hear the Black Mamba in his shelter talking with Bundi, their voices low. She was falling asleep as a radio handset crackled to life. She half-listened to the Black Mamba barking orders; muddled messages about a bluebird arriving in the morning. A bluebird with arms, carrying a white lioness.

CHAPTER TWELVE

imara

The bluebird was a helicopter. It wasn't like a bird at all. It buzzed above the camp like an outsized shiny blue beetle. All the Mambas and the miners stopped what they were doing and craned their necks to look up at it.

Imara had seen the white helicopters of the United Nations patrolling the skies, but they had always stayed in the far, far distance. They never came this close. Imara covered her ears as the helicopter clattered out of the thin morning mist to land on the cleared and level ground. The air pulsed with the sound of it. She leaned into the downdraft from the rotor blades, which flattened the grasses and sent loose mud and stones into the air.

Saka stood beside her, pointing into the cockpit. "Mzungus," he said. "White people."

Three white-skinned figures sat inside the helicopter, their faces half hidden by their sunglasses and helmets. They waited until the rotor blades slowed, the whirling blur separating into four long blades. The whine of engines faded and the pilot climbed out, holding the door for the other two passengers. The first was a big man, red faced, with a fuzz of grayish hair. His round stomach stuck out over his faded jeans. The second passenger was tall and slim-hipped. Imara watched the passenger slide the helmet off to release a mane of long hair, the color of the sun.

Imara stared.

This mzungu was a woman.

Imara watched the Black Mamba walk into the clearing. He was clean-shaven and had changed out of his T-shirt and combat trousers into a military uniform, decorated with medals. As he passed, Imara could smell the false flower scent of soap on his skin. He preened himself, brushing the creases out of his trousers and running his tongue along his teeth. He looked smaller to Imara. Ordinary. Weakened. Just a man. A man pretending to be a king.

The gray-haired mzungu's eyes were hidden behind his sunglasses. He walked with a long swagger as if he owned the mine. But Imara could tell he was nervous. He chewed on gum, his jaw muscles working hard. His fingers twitched where a pistol lay outlined beneath his shirt.

The woman was different. She shook out her mane of hair, put her hand on her hip, and surveyed the mine, looking down her long thin nose. She pushed her sunglasses on top of her head, revealing eyes the color of a pale morning sky. She swept them across the Mambas, standing in a ragged circle, finally coming to rest on the Black Mamba, with Bundi and Rat at his sides.

"Well," she announced, "I thought I had come to the camp of a great leader, not a rag-tag army. I have come to meet the Black Mamba." She spoke French, the business language of the Congo.

The Black Mamba gave Bundi a shove and nodded toward the woman. Bundi ran his finger around his collar and wiped sweat from his forehead. He shuffled forward. "The Black Mamba welcomes the White Lioness to his camp." He held out his hand. "Please come this way; the Black Mamba would like to offer you to sit with him and take some coffee."

The White Lioness walked past Bundi to the Black Mamba. She paused, looking directly in his eyes. "Come," she said. "Let's talk some business."

Close up, Imara could see the White Lioness was older than she first thought. Her face was pale, the color of blood-tinged milk, and her skin looked pinched and lacked the smoothness of youth. Fine lines ran across her forehead and around her down-turned mouth. She wore a simple white shirt and khaki trousers, yet her lips and nails were painted red. A diamond pendant hung from a gold chain around her neck.

Imara couldn't stop staring. The demon inside her was transfixed too. Never had she seen a woman in control of men before. The White Lioness had neither the Black Mamba's strength, nor a weapon of any sort, but it was clear to Imara that what this woman possessed was power.

The Black Mamba snapped his fingers. "Imara, bring coffee to my tent."

Imara nodded, aware the White Lioness's eyes lingered on her scar.

Imara filled the pan with fresh water and stoked the fire. She added crushed coffee beans and sugar cane into the pan and let it boil to a treacly liquid, just how the Black Mamba liked his coffee.

She carried the pan of coffee and separate cups to the Black Mamba's shelter and placed them on an upturned beer crate, keeping her face down as she poured the hot drink. She backed away, turning to leave.

"Wait," said the White Lioness.

Imara stopped.

The White Lioness got to her feet and stood in front of her. "So, is this the Spirit Child I hear people speak about?" Imara flinched as the White Lioness reached out to touch the long scar on her face.

"Pity," she said, putting her hand beneath Imara's chin and pushing her face up for a closer look. "I expect you were once such a pretty child."

Imara pulled her face away.

The White Lioness smiled. She leaned forward and whispered, "We are alike, you and me. Men fear us, and that gives us power."

Imara remained silent, but the demon rose up inside.

She likes you. She sees your power.

The White Lioness moved her face closer so that Imara could see tiny flecks of darker blue in her pale irises. "I am told that to look at you is to see your own death. Tell me, Spirit Child, how am I to die?"

Tell her what she wants to hear.

Imara stared back. "You will die rich," she said, "in a bed of gold and diamonds."

The White Lioness laughed. "You flatter me." She sipped her coffee, rolling the sticky liquid around her teeth. "But I have no interest in people who flatter me. What else do you see?"

This woman is like the Black Mamba. She cares for no one but herself. People die because of her. Play her game, Imara; make her fear you.

Imara frowned. "You will die alone," she said, "stained with blood that is not your own."

The White Lioness raised an eyebrow and paused. "Well, thank God for that." She reached for a cigarette in her pocket and lit it, drawing in heavily and then breathing out, creating a screen of smoke between them.

The White Lioness looked across at the Black Mamba, her lip curled up in amusement. "Is this your secret weapon in the jungle? A Spirit Child? What else do you have? Voodoo dolls and witch doctors? Is this all you have here?" She flicked ash at him. "Isn't it time to catch up with the modern world?"

She is powerful, whispered the demon. **See how she plays with the Mamba like a mouse between her paws. Stay and watch, Imara. See who wins this battle.**

Imara waited. The White Lioness could pretend she wasn't afraid, but the gray-haired mzungu did not dare look Imara in the eye.

The White Lioness continued her game. "Is this all you have for me? A few spells and witchcraft, and a few boys with snake tattoos running in the woods?"

The Black Mamba frowned. Imara could see he gripped the coffee cup tightly in his hand. "Bundi," he ordered, "show the White Lioness what we have here."

Bundi left the shelter and heaved in a large sack, straining under the weight. The Black Mamba reached in and picked out a lump of gray rock and threw it at the White Lioness's feet. "Coltan," he said. "You will not find a better grade of coltan anywhere else in Africa."

The White Lioness picked up the rock and handed it to the gray-haired mzungu. "Clarkson, take a look at this."

Clarkson rolled it in his fingers. He took a hand lens from his pocket and peered at the rock. Imara leaned forward to see. The rock looked larger beneath the small glass lens, picking out all the small details she couldn't see by eye.

Clarkson nodded in approval.

"I have many clients who all want this coltan," said the White Lioness. "How can I be sure you can supply me with a steady trade?"

"Have you brought me what I asked for?" said the Black Mamba. "We need weapons to defend the mine."

The White Lioness studied him. "In the helicopter I have arms for you. I have Kalashnikov rifles and three rocket launchers and ammunition. I have also brought the other things you asked for: rice, beer, the oil-fired generator, and the chainsaws." She leaned back and crossed one leg over the other. "I can supply your every need if you can supply me with the coltan."

"We need to work out our price," said the Black Mamba, glancing at Bundi.

The White Lioness smiled, showing a line of perfect white teeth. "I decide the price," she said. She pushed a piece of paper toward the Black Mamba, who studied it, squinting at the wiggles on the paper. He handed it to Bundi, who muttered into the Black Mamba's ear.

"It is not enough," said the Black Mamba. "I know many clients willing to pay more for my coltan."

The White Lioness shrugged her shoulders. "Then we do not have a deal," she said. She stood up to leave, dropping the cigarette end on the ground and crushing it beneath her foot. "But I ask you, do you really want to sell your coltan in the backstreets like some small-town miner? I doubt many of your other clients have a helicopter to transport the coltan out of the Congo."

The Black Mamba picked up another piece of coltan rock and twirled it in his palm. "Wait . . . ," he said.

The White Lioness turned. She lit another cigarette, a smile playing on her lips as she inhaled.

"I need to think," said the Black Mamba.

The White Lioness leaned toward him. "I have many, many clients who want your coltan," she repeated. "My clients are from some of the biggest electronics companies in America, Europe, and Asia." She paused. "I represent the world. Remember that," she said, blowing out a halo of smoke. "Hold that thought in your head before you turn me down. I represent the rest of the *world*."

The Black Mamba stood up and glanced at Bundi.

"Black Mamba," said the White Lioness, her voice suddenly soft. She smiled at him. "I can make you a big man, a rich man." She ran her eyes from his head to his worn leather boots caked in mud. "I can make you a king. A coltan king. Think about it. If I can have your coltan, you can keep your kingdom."

The Black Mamba swallowed hard and nodded. "We have a deal," he said.

The White Lioness shook her hair and smiled. She examined her nails and tutted. "But there is such bad press about coltan in the news these days. It is such a bore. My clients will want to be reassured that armed gangs and rebel groups do not control the mine. You are a considerate man, Black Mamba. Can you provide documentation that your coltan is conflict free?"

The Black Mamba stroked his chin. "I know a man who can," he said.

"Good." The White Lioness smiled. She sat back down. "Now," she said, holding out her hands, "the question is, are you a man of your word? Have you found what I asked for in return? Do you have it here for me now?

The Black Mamba swigged the last dregs of his coffee. "Soon," he said.

The White Lioness raised an eyebrow. "You do not have it?"

"I will have your gorilla baby soon."

The White Lioness nodded. "Next time," she said, "have it for me when I come, or we do not have a deal."

gorilla

Hisani's son pulled a piece of bamboo, stripping the hard outer covering and chewing the sweet inside. He stole glances at the silverback. Hodari was agitated. He patrolled the group, keeping the family close. One of the Watchers had followed them through the day's brightness and slept near them in the dark. The Tall Ape had pushed them higher into the mountain, away from the bamboo on the lower slopes.

Hodari had mock-charged him, with roars and short barks, but the Watcher did not challenge the silverback. He lay quiet and still, and kept his eyes down, but he didn't move away.

All day the Watcher had moved them upward. Hodari pulled at vines and stripped bark, glaring at the Tall Ape intruder who forced his family to move away from their favorite food.

The Watcher settled with them for their afternoon rest. Hisani's son could see the other gorillas pull leaves around themselves and doze, belch-grunting in contentment after a morning's foraging. He watched his mother chew on a leaf, her eyes closing. She flicked at insects buzzing around her head and shifted to find a comfortable sleeping place in the leaves. Her stomach rumbled with food in her belly.

Even Hodari began to settle. He sat back, casting his eyes across his family, rolling nettles in a ball to hide the stinging hairs before putting it into his mouth while one of females groomed him. She ran her fingers through his fur, picking bugs and flakes of dead skin.

Only Enzi, the blackback, had energy to play. He chased Hisani's son round and round, mock-charging and slapping his hands on his chest. But even Enzi began to tire and he too settled down to rest, yawning and scratching his belly.

Hisani's son looked around for another playmate. He

stripped a small branch from a sapling and charged in a circle, beating the ground with it. The other gorillas yawned in the sun and ignored him. He slapped the sapling in Enzi's face, but Enzi grunted and turned away to sleep. Hisani's son gave up. He chewed a leaf and tried to curl up next to his mother, but he didn't feel tired. His mind raced and his limbs felt fidgety and restless. He sat up and looked around his sleeping family. No one wanted to play. Even the Watcher was sleeping, his eyes closed and his mouth wide open.

Hisani's son glanced slyly at his mother. She never let him near the Tall Apes, but right now she was asleep. Right now, she couldn't stop him. He crept toward the Watcher for a better view. The Watcher's head had lolled back and Hisani's son could see right into the Tall Ape's mouth, at the pink inside and the rows of small white teeth.

He reached out to touch the Watcher's face. It was smooth and warm and hairless. He pulled at the soft coverings the Tall Apes wrapped around their furless bodies and pushed a finger up one of the Tall Ape's nostrils, but the Tall Ape batted him away, turning over in sleep. Hisani's son sat back down, scratching at his fur, pondering what to do.

He reached out for the wad of square white leaves that lay beneath the Watcher's hand. He tore one leaf and put it in his mouth. It tasted of dry bark and stuck around his teeth and beneath his tongue. He tore out another, listening to the dry ripping sound. He could see Enzi stirring. If Enzi woke, he'd want this wad of leaves and would take them away. Now that he had them to himself, Hisani's son wasn't going to let them go. He clambered up into the trees, higher and higher, until the branches bowed beneath him. Enzi would be too heavy for these branches. He wouldn't reach him here.

Hisani's son settled in a crook between the branches and tore out another white leaf and chewed it, turning it to sticky pulp inside his mouth. Small birds hopped along beside him, picking out insects from the moss with their tiny beaks.

Sunlight filtered through the leaves and warmed his back. Hisani's son could feel his eyes begin to close. He could go back down to join his family, but he was comfortable up in the tree. He was becoming big and brave, like Enzi. He no longer needed to be clutching to his mother all the time. He was drifting into sleep when the small birds left in a flurry of wings, disappearing into thicker foliage. Hisani's son sat up and looked around to see what had startled them, but there were no snakes or monkeys in the branches. Below him, the other gorillas hadn't stirred. Maybe it was nothing. Maybe there was no danger. But then Hisani's son caught a glimpse of a shadow sliding in the undergrowth. He leaned out and looked down. A figure was downwind from Hodari. A small Tall Ape, a young one, was creeping through the leaves. It came so close to the Watcher that it could almost touch it. It rose up and looked at the other gorillas too. Hodari stirred, batting an insect with his hand.

Hisani's son watched as the small Tall Ape slipped away as silently as he had come. But the small birds didn't return. The forest was still and silent. Watching.

Waiting.

Hisani's son gripped the tree. His fur prickled along his back. He didn't want to be on his own anymore. He wanted his mother. He wanted her arms around him.

He dropped the wad of flat leaves and watched them fall, batting against the branches, spiraling downward toward the ground.

Hodari woke. He sat up, his eyes wide and fixed beyond the falling flat white leaves. He barked a warning bark. The other gorillas stirred, getting to their feet. The pungent smell of fear was in the air. Hodari and Enzi were facing a threat that Hisani's son couldn't see. The silverback was standing upright, his teeth bared. The other gorillas were moving away. Hisani's son could hear his mother's sharp call, a cry for him to find her. He started to slide down the tree. He wanted to be with her, to be held by her and feel her warm fur against his skin. He wanted to clamber onto her back and be carried by her, but his mother was moving away with the others. Hisani's son gave a shriek, a cry for her, but it was drowned by the sound of a fire-stick, its thunder ripping apart the air.

Hisani's son lost his grip and felt himself falling, falling, falling, head over foot, round and round and round, thumping from branch to branch. In his spinning world he saw the great silverback lying on his back, eyes blank and unseeing, and the Watcher standing, arms widespread in front of three new Tall Apes, as if he was trying to protect the gorillas too. But the Watcher's eyes were wide with fear.

The forest was filled with the screams of gorillas and new

Tall Apes. The sharp stench of smoke hung in the air.

Another shot splintered the forest.

Hisani's son screamed for his mother as he landed on the soft ground. He scrambled up, but felt small thin hands grab him and wrap him up in darkness. They clamped around him, holding him tighter and tighter.

He tried to call for his mother but he couldn't breathe.

He couldn't move.

Bright stars swirled around him and he felt as if he was falling through an endless empty sky, far away from his mother, into the deepest, darkest night.

CHAPTER THIRTEEN

bobo

Tsk, Bobo, do your homework. You are getting under my feet."

Bobo paced up and down the room. "What time will Kambale get here?"

Mama looked up at him. "I don't know. It could be this evening, it could be tomorrow."

"I'll wait."

"Bobo, you have homework, and I have Mr. Shabani's accounts to finish."

"Papa has been away nearly a week now," said Bobo. "Seven days! It is too long."

Mama put down her pen. "Kambale will come back when he has some information. He and the other rangers have gone to find him. Papa is probably still moving the Tumaini group to this side of the mountain."

Bobo shook his head. "Kambale said he lost contact with Papa two days ago."

"Kambale also said that the batteries in the radio had probably stopped working."

"But, Mama," said Bobo, "what if—"

"Bobo," she snapped. "What if . . . what if . . . ? What if . . . ? What if you do not go to school, eh? What if I do not get these accounts done by the end of the day? We still have things to do while we wait for news."

Bobo turned and paced the room. Up and down. Up and down. He listened to the scratching of his mother's pen on the paper and the sound of his sister singing in the next room.

Mama slammed her pen down. "Would you stop pacing? You are wearing a hole in the floor."

Bobo stopped and stared out the window.

"Go to your room, Bobo. You are making me restless."

"I can see Kambale," said Bobo, pressing his face against the shutters. "He is coming down the road."

Mama took a sharp breath. "Are you sure it's him?"

Bobo nodded.

Mama stood up, knocking back her chair. Her pen clattered to the floor. She joined Bobo at the window, her hands gripped tight together in prayer.

Bobo tried to read Kambale's face, but Kambale kept his head bowed as he walked toward the house.

"Let him in," said Mama, her voice a hoarse whisper.

Kambale walked through the door and took his beret off, holding it in his hands.

"Please," said Mama, "take a seat."

Kambale sat down at the table, but would not look Bobo or his mother in the eye. Bobo moved closer.

"Bobo, leave us please," said Mama.

Bobo pulled up a seat. "I will stay. I have to find out what Kambale has to say soon enough."

Kambale nodded and let Bobo join them at the table. "I'm afraid I have bad news."

Mama gripped the table. "Is . . . is he dead?"

Kambale shook his head. "We don't know. We don't know where he is."

"But he is with the gorillas," blurted Bobo. "You know that."

Kambale frowned. "The Tumaini group was attacked. Hodari, the great silverback, has been shot."

Bobo felt bile rise into his throat. "Hodari is dead?"

Kambale nodded. "We found a bullet wound in his chest."

"So where is Papa?" said Bobo. "He would have protected the gorillas."

"We don't know where he is," said Kambale. "All we have found is his field notes scattered on the ground."

"Maybe he is with the rest of the gorillas?" said Bobo.

Kambale sighed. "We found them farther up the mountain huddled together, not knowing what to do. We couldn't see Hisani's son, either. We think the rebels have him. They often target the silverback to get to the babies."

"But what about Papa?" insisted Bobo. "Didn't you find anything else?"

Kambale shook his head. "Nothing."

Mama leaned forward and gripped Kambale's arm. "But who is looking for him now?"

Kambale couldn't meet her eyes. "The rebels are in the forest. We heard shots from the valley. It was not safe for us to stay."

Mama shook her head from side to side. "So what do we do now?"

Kambale took her hand. "We wait. Maybe he is hiding in the mountains. Maybe he is finding another way back to us."

Bobo banged his fist in the table. "No. Papa

would have defended the gorillas. He would have stayed with them after Hodari was killed."

Kambale opened his mouth as if he had an answer, but then shook his head. "I know," he said. "That is my thought too. Bobo, I wish I had the answers to your questions, but I do not."

CHAPTER FOURTEEN

bobo

The next day at school, Bobo couldn't concentrate. The other pupils left him alone with his thoughts. He overheard some talk of the Black Mamba and the Spirit Child. But what had happened to his father? Bobo tried to run through every scenario in his head; his father tracking the gorillas and the rebels closing in. What would Papa have done? Had he defended the gorillas? Had he tried to radio for help? Had he been injured? Was he trying to find his way home? And why didn't the rebels take the silverback? They were known to take gorillas for meat. Maybe Papa had scared them off. So where was he now? Nothing made sense. His mind whirred with thoughts all day until Lamu joined him on his way back home.

Lamu was silent at first, bouncing his ball along the road, only stopping to wait while Bobo picked his sister up from school on the way.

"My father says your papa is a brave man," said Lamu.

Bobo nodded. He felt tears burn in his eyes.

"He says if anyone deserves a medal for defending the gorillas, your papa does."

Bobo smiled. He knew Lamu was trying to cheer him up, but it was a nice thing to say anyway.

"Look," said Lamu, pointing to Bobo's house. "See, the police are at your house now. That looks like the police chief's car. Maybe he has come with your father's medal."

Bobo looked up and stopped. A sleek black car with blacked out windows and two police motorbikes were parked outside Bobo's house. Bobo felt sick inside. "What's he doing here?"

"Maybe Papa has come home," burst out his sister. She ran ahead, her feet flying up behind her.

"Wait," called Bobo. He was running too. Maybe his sister was right. It seemed impossible to believe but maybe Papa had come home. Maybe he had seen off the rebels and was a hero. Maybe the police chief was here to give Papa his medal.

Bobo burst through the door with his sister.

The chief of police and two officials were in the house. Mama was sitting at the table, her head in her hands. Kambale was standing next to her, his beret clutched against his chest.

There was no sign of Papa.

Bobo looked around. "Is there any news?"

Kambale stepped forward. "Bobo, this is Charles Mutombo, the chief of police."

Bobo looked at the man and nodded. Charles Mutombo was a big man. Solid. Medals decorated the lapel of his blue uniform. He stood in the middle of the room with his arms folded, feet slightly apart. The police chief was an important man. What was he doing here? Bobo couldn't see behind the dark glasses but he could feel the eyes of the police chief looking right at him.

"We have news of your father," said Mutombo.

Bobo glanced at Kambale, but Kambale couldn't look him in the eye.

Bobo felt his chest tighten, as if he'd forgotten how to breathe. "Is Papa dead?"

Mama covered her face with her hands.

Bobo looked at Kambale. "What is it? What has happened?"

Kambale just shook his head slowly from side to side.

Mutombo removed his glasses and pushed them in his top pocket. He reached out and put a hand on Bobo's shoulder. "It is much worse, Bobo. Much worse."

Bobo swallowed hard. "What has happened?"

Mutombo shook his head. "Your father has joined the rebels."

CHAPTER FIFTEEN

bobo

Bobo felt the world fall away beneath him. "No!" Mama began to sob and held Bobo's sister close to her.

"No," said Bobo again. "Papa wouldn't do that. Tell him, Kambale. Tell the police chief that Papa is a good man."

Kambale stared hard at the ground. "I find it hard to believe myself," he said.

Bobo spun around to face the police chief. "No!" he shouted. "My father would not do that."

Mutombo unfolded his arms and hooked his

fingers in his belt. "We have good evidence that your father is one of the rebels now."

Bobo slammed his hands down on the table. "What evidence?" he shouted.

The police chief glared at him.

Silence filled the room.

Mama stood up and pulled Bobo's sleeve. "Tsk, Bobo, sit down. Do not talk to the police chief like that."

Mutombo's eyes lingered on Bobo. "You would do well to listen to your mother. Maybe you have the same lack of respect for authority as your father."

Bobo stared at the ground, clenching his fists, his body burning with anger.

"But as you asked," Mutombo continued, "we intercepted a call made on his radio. He made a call to the rebels to tell them the location of the gorillas."

Bobo glanced at Kambale, but Kambale wouldn't meet his eyes.

The police chief walked to the door, but turned before he left. "Your father has destroyed the reputation of the rangers and the reputation of the park. He has put the gorillas at risk. He knows the mountains better than anyone. Now that he has joined the rebels, it has become too dangerous to patrol the park. I will have to stop all ranger patrols there until we know it is safe."

Bobo waited until he heard the police chief's car roar away. He kicked the door and spun around to face Kambale and his mother. "Papa would not do such a thing. He wouldn't."

Kambale nodded. "There has been a mistake. Maybe the rebels took his radio from him and made that call."

Bobo gripped Kambale's arm. "Yes. That must be it. Papa did not make that call. We must tell the police chief. We must make him understand."

Kambale sighed. "But it is hard to prove and people want someone to blame. We have not found your father. All we have found is his field notes scattered on the ground."

Bobo snatched at thoughts. "What about his rucksack, with his stuff? What about his camera? Maybe he has photos of the rebels?"

Kambale shook his head. "We didn't find anything else. That is the problem."

"So what can we do?" said Bobo.

Kambale shrugged his shoulders. "We wait," he said, "and hope. Maybe we will hear more news. It is all we can do."

Bobo clung to Kambale. "But you must help us. Go and see the police chief. Tell him Papa is innocent."

Kambale put his hand on Bobo's shoulder. "Bobo, my priority is to protect the park. It will be hard enough, now that we are not even allowed inside." He put on his beret and guided Lamu outside. Lamu clutched his ball and didn't look at Bobo. He kept close to his father as if he couldn't wait to get out of the house.

Bobo closed his eyes. His head felt light and dizzy. He knelt down and touched his palms to the floor to stop the world from reeling around him.

Last week his father had filled the room. It had breathed with his presence. But now the room, like Bobo, felt wide and empty.

Bobo opened his eyes and glanced at Mama. She had wiped her tears and had started working through Mr. Shabani's accounts, her pen making notes and marks in the margins. "Mama! What are you doing? We need to prove Papa is innocent."

Mama looked up at him. "I need to earn money to put food on the table."

Bobo narrowed his eyes. "You think Papa is guilty too!" Mama twisted the pen round and round in her fingers. "Of course I don't. But I need to keep us together until Papa returns. What can I do? You heard Kambale. All we can do now is wait. Wait and hope."

At school the next day, Bobo knew the other children and teachers were avoiding him. There were no more sympathetic stares or quiet words of support, just hushed whispers when he left a room. When he collected his sister from her school, the parents didn't look at him or ask after Mama. Only Lamu walked with him home from school.

Bobo pushed his hands deep in his pockets. "Everyone thinks my father has joined the rebels."

Lamu kicked his soccer ball ahead of him. "My father doesn't."

"But the police chief thinks he has. The police chief doesn't know my father. If he did, he would know that my father would give his life for the gorillas. I need to prove to him that my father is innocent."

"How will you do that?"

Bobo shrugged his shoulders. He gazed into the distance to the mountains rising up into the sky. "Someone, somewhere must know where my father is. People don't just disappear."

Lamu stopped outside Bobo's house. "Let me know if I can help."

Bobo nodded, took his sister's hand, and stepped through the door.

● ● ●

Inside the house, Bobo's sister gripped his hand and stopped. Pots and pans lay piled by the door. Rolled blankets and bags filled with clothes were stacked together. The baby was lying on a blanket crying, his face creased in frustration.

"Mama?" called Bobo.

Bobo's mother appeared from the small yard outside. "Mama, what is happening?"

Mama wiped sweat from her forehead. She picked up the baby, rocking him gently, stroking his head. "I'm sorry, Bobo."

Bobo stared around him. "Why are all our things packed? Are we leaving?"

Mama nodded. "We must go to my mother's village for a while."

"For good?"

Mama held the baby close. Bobo's sister wrapped her arms around Mama's waist. "I don't know."

"No," said Bobo.

"Word has spread quickly about Papa. Mr. Shabani says he does not need my work. We don't have your father's pay. People are angry. They say Papa is a shame to the community. We cannot stay here in town. We will get the bus first thing in the morning."

Bobo shook his head. "But this is home. And what about school? Papa said I must go to school." Bobo knew this would hurt his mother, but in that moment he didn't care.

Mama frowned. "We will see. Maybe there is a school in my mother's village. But we will have to help in the fields as there will be more mouths to feed."

Bobo paced in circles around her. "But when Papa comes back, how will he find us?"

"He knows the village where my mother lives."

Bobo dropped his school bag on the floor. "I'm not leaving. I'm staying right here."

"Bobo, my son," said Mama, her voice weary. "This is not our home anymore. We have to leave. We have no choice."

Bobo changed out of his school uniform, folding the blue shirt and black shorts on his bed. This was the bed where Papa had sat beside him at bedtime, telling him stories of the animals in the park and the people who lived around it. This was where Mama had stroked his head with a cool cloth whenever he had a fever. But now the bed was stripped bare of sheets and blankets and the small cupboard where he stored his clothes was empty. It felt as if he was shutting a door to his past life and moving on. Moving on, leaving with unanswered questions, leaving without his father. Bobo reached into his school bag and pulled out an exercise book and pen. He tore out a page and began to write, an idea forming in his mind and spilling out as words. He pulled on the shirt and long trousers his mother had left on the bed, tucked the piece of paper in his shirt pocket, and went to find her.

"I am going to see Lamu, to say good-bye," he said.

Mama looked up from feeding the baby. She nodded. "Don't be long. Make sure you are back before dark."

Bobo pulled on his shoes and paused in the doorway. "Mama?"

Mama looked up at him. But Bobo just stood there.

"What is it, Bobo?"

Bobo picked at the flaking paint on the door. "Nothing," he said. He had wanted to tell her that he loved her, but if he had, he knew he wouldn't have been able to leave. He closed the door and left, without saying a last good-bye.

He kept up a steady jog across the town to Lamu's house, where he found him playing soccer in the street with his brother and their friends.

"Hey, Bobo," said Lamu, running up to him. "What's up?"

Bobo pulled him away. "I have come to say good-bye. We have to leave town in the morning, to go to my mother's village."

Lamu's eyes fell to the ground. "I've heard. My mother told me."

Bobo straightened his back. "But I'm not going with them."

Lamu looked up. "You're not?"

Bobo shook his head. "Lamu, you said you would help me."

Lamu frowned. "I know, and I will if I can."

"Then give this to my mother," Bobo said, pulling the piece of paper from his pocket.

Lamu backed away, eyeing the letter suspiciously. "What's in it?"

"It is a letter saying why I am going to the mountains."

Lamu shook his head from side to side. "No way. You're crazy, Bobo. You'll get yourself killed. People will say you have gone to join the rebels too."

Bobo pressed the letter into Lamu's hand. "You mustn't tell . . . not until I'm long gone."

Lamu stared hard at the envelope. "Bobo . . . I can't. . . ."

"You promised me, Lamu," said Bobo. "I need you to be the one to tell everyone that I haven't joined the rebels."

Lamu took the letter from Bobo, holding it with

the very tips of his fingers. "So what *do* I tell them?"

Bobo turned and fixed his eyes on the distant mountains. "Tell them I have gone to find my father. Tell them I have gone to prove my father is an innocent man."

CHAPTER SIXTEEN

imara

Imara pushed the door to the cramped makeshift hut she'd insisted the Mambas build for her. The hut had been put together from rough-hewn planks of wood and covered with plastic sheeting and leaves. There were large holes, but the hut kept most of the rain and insects outside. She put her back against the door, shutting out the drizzle and evening light. Since the White Lioness's visit, the forest had roared with the sound of chainsaws. The Mambas had worked quickly, cutting more trees, clearing the forest around the camp for charcoal and timber. The Black Mamba had his own wooden cabin too. It was set higher up on the slopes over-looking the open mine. It had a table and stools made from wide tree stumps. The Black Mamba's sleeping mattress was set onto a raised platform to keep it off the damp ground. He and Bundi were the only ones to have such luxury in the forest. The rest of the men still slept in hammocks or on the ground beneath stretched tarpaulin.

But Imara was relieved to have a small hut of her own. If she spread her arms, she could almost touch all the walls, but it was her space, away from the men. It was somewhere she could keep her sleeping mat and a roof over her head. She rolled out her sleeping mat on the damp ground and lay down, pulling her blanket around her. She closed her eyes, trying to reach the place between wake and sleep where the woman with the coffee-colored skin might find her. She inhaled deeply, hoping to smell the scent of sweet ripe mangos that came before her.

Shouts came from the camp, pulling Imara from

her slumber. She sat up and crawled to the door, opening it just a crack to peer out.

In the firelight she saw Rat, Saka, and two of the Mambas returning from their trip into the forest. Rat dropped two sacks to the ground. He picked one up and held it high. "Come and see," he called. "See what I have brought back from the forest."

Imara could see the other Mambas crowd around him.

The Black Mamba walked out from the shadows. "Have you got what I wanted?" he said.

Rat reached into one sack and pulled something out. At first, all Imara could see was a long arm covered in dark fur. As Rat pulled, the arm was followed by the rest of the creature it belonged to. A young gorilla. Rat held it up and grinned, triumphant. The gorilla's head flopped forward, the other arm and legs hung loosely by its side.

The Black Mamba walked around Rat in a slow circle. "This gorilla is no use to me dead."

The Rat jabbed the young gorilla in the stomach.

The gorilla flinched, curling its legs up to its chest. "See, it's alive," said Rat.

The Black Mamba pulled up its head. "It is sick," he said.

"Just tired," assured Rat. He dropped the gorilla on the ground, where it lay, unmoving. "We have been walking all day with it inside this sack. It needs food."

The Black Mamba stroked his chin and turned to Saka. "Where did you find it?"

Saka pointed to the mountains silhouetted against the night sky. "Higher up there, moving toward the other side."

"I killed the silverback," blurted out Rat, keen to have his moment of glory. "He charged at me thumping his chest. Big as two men."

"Where is it now?" asked the Black Mamba.

"We had to leave it," said Rat. "There were rangers protecting the gorillas."

"Many?" said the Black Mamba.

"Ten, maybe twenty," said Rat.

The Black Mamba turned to Saka again. "How many rangers?"

"We saw only one."

Rat glared at Saka. "We dealt with the ranger. Here," he said, nodding to the other sack on the ground. "I have his stuff."

Imara watched the Black Mamba tip the contents of the sack on the floor. He picked through them, turning things over in his hands. Imara strained her eyes, but it was too dark to see what he was looking at.

"Well done," said the Black Mamba, turning to Saka. "I reward loyalty and bravery." He took Saka's arm and pushed back the sleeve of his shirt to his elbow. He traced an S shape with his finger across the skin. "Soon, Imara will mark you with the sign of the Black Mamba." He smiled, showing his gold tooth. "Well done, Saka. Soon, you will be one of us."

Imara watched Saka clutch his arm and move away into the shadows to seek out Frog. Rat used the moment to rummage through the contents of the second sack and slink away into the night. Imara tried to see where he had gone and what he was carrying close to his chest, but Rat had already disappeared into the dark spaces between the trees.

"Bundi," the Black Mamba called. "Come and see what to do with this gorilla."

Bundi walked over and crouched down, pushing his glasses farther up his nose to examine the gorilla.

"The gorilla is sick," said the Black Mamba. "What do we do?"

Bundi turned the gorilla over, lifting its arms and legs. He wrinkled his nose at the foul-smelling diarrhea smeared around its backside. "This gorilla needs medicine."

"Then get some," snapped the Black Mamba.

Bundi disappeared into the Black Mamba's cabin and returned with three sachets of medicine and a bottle of water. Imara had seen Bundi use the medicine to treat Mambas for the sickness that was sweeping through the mines. Bundi mixed the powder from one of the sachets in the water and shook it. He poured the liquid into the gorilla's mouth, but the young gorilla spluttered and choked and didn't swallow.

Bundi tutted and shook his head. "I am not a doctor," he said. "But I think this gorilla is too young, too sick. I don't think he will survive the night."

The Black Mamba hit the ground with his fist. He sought out Rat in the shadows. "Rat, where are you?"

"Here," said Rat. He appeared out of the forest puffing and out of breath. Imara noticed he was now empty-handed.

"Rat," ordered the Black Mamba, "this gorilla is no use to us. You must go back and find an older one."

Rat swallowed hard. "This was the only young one. The rest were adults."

"Saka," yelled the Black Mamba, "is this true?"

Saka nodded. "It was the only one."

The Black Mamba turned back to the gorilla

again. It lay limp and lifeless on the ground. "We have a problem. The White Lioness wants this gorilla. How do we keep it alive until she comes back?"

Rat turned to face Imara's hut and she shrank back, feeling his eyes search for her. "Ask the Spirit Child. If she can talk to the spirits, surely she can use her great powers to keep this gorilla alive."

Imara felt the demon rise inside her. **Be careful, Imara. Rat is challenging your power.**

The Black Mamba turned to face the hut. "Imara!" he called out.

Don't go, don't go.

"IMARA!" he called a second time.

Imara slid out from the hut and walked slowly across to the fire. The men parted to allow her through. She looked down at the small gorilla curled on the floor and the demon recoiled inside her.

It is sick, Imara. It will die. You can do nothing for it.

But Imara couldn't pull her eyes away.

Don't touch it. Say it is evil. Tell them to kill it now.

Imara knelt down beside it and lifted the gorilla's arm from its face.

It turned its head toward her and Imara found herself falling deep into its amber eyes. The young gorilla was barely holding on to life, yet it held Imara there. It blinked and blinked again. It seemed to look beyond her scar and beyond the demon, to some forgotten place inside, a place somewhere just beyond her memory. Imara felt a small glow ignite within her chest and flare like a fire taking hold of the dry grasses. It spread outward, filling her with warmth.

She reached down to scoop the young gorilla in her arms.

Don't look at it, Imara. Don't look.

"Hush now," whispered Imara to the demon.

Imara! screamed the demon. **They are all watching you. Don't let them see me.**

"Hush, now," Imara repeated, speaking softly

to the demon. "Go. Leave me for a while."

Imara held the gorilla close. She stood up, rocking it gently in her arms, humming a song. She ran her fingers through the coarse hairs on its back. She felt its long fingers grip onto her clothes and pull itself closer. Its small heart beat against hers. She buried her face in its fur, smelling the dampness of the forest. She felt the demon flow out of her, through her breath, her fingertips, and the pores of her skin. The demon left her quiet and still, her mind clear of voices.

Imara felt the Black Mamba and his men watching her, transfixed, as she cradled the gorilla baby against her. She became aware of some deep power between her and the gorilla that held them, watching, as if it stirred some deep forgotten part of them too.

The gorilla reached up and traced his long finger down Imara's scar, resting his finger on her lip.

The Black Mamba broke the silence. "Imara, can you save it?"

Imara pulled the gorilla against her chest, shielding him within her arms.

"Of course," she said. "I am the Spirit Child." She turned to face the men. "I name him Kitwana. The one who lives."

CHAPTER SEVENTEEN

imara

*I*mara scooped up the two unopened sachets of medicine and walked away through the line of men, with Kitwana in her arms. She stepped into her hut and shut the door, wrapping Kitwana and herself in darkness.

Stupid girl. You can't save it. The gorilla will die and the Black Mamba will see your powers are weakened.

It was too dark to see anything in the hut, but Imara could feel Kitwana's short shallow breaths. His palms were cold to the touch and his stomach

148

felt hollow and empty, yet he gripped Imara's hand in his as if he was clinging to life. Imara leaned against the walls of her hut and closed her eyes. She had promised she could look after this gorilla, but she didn't even know what to feed him. Bundi was probably right. Kitwana wouldn't survive the night.

She lay Kitwana on the ground and hid the unopened sachets of medicine between the sheets of tarpaulin on her roof.

"Pssst!"

Imara heard a soft knock at the door and Saka's whispered voice. "It's me, me and Frog. We have food for the gorilla baby."

Imara opened the door. Frog stood in front of her holding a small paraffin lamp in one hand and two bananas in the other. Saka held up an empty wooden beer crate.

"You can use this crate as a bed for Kitwana," said Saka. "See, I have lined it with leaves, like he would sleep in the forest."

Imara took the crate and put it on the floor of her hut.

"And some bananas," said Frog. "So he can eat."

Imara nodded, took the lamp and bananas, and closed the door on Saka and Frog.

"Imara?" whispered Saka from the other side of the door. "Do you want us to help?"

"Go away," growled Imara. "I can do this myself."

She placed the lamp in the corner of the hut where it threw long shadows of her against the wall. She lifted Kitwana onto her lap and tried to get him to eat one of the bananas, but each time he turned his head away. She tried to press mashed banana in his mouth, but Kitwana pushed it back out with his tongue. It squeezed between his teeth and dribbled down his chin. She half-wished she'd asked Saka and Frog to help, but knew the demon wouldn't allow her to rely on anyone.

"Come on," she whispered, pressing more squashed banana into Kitwana's mouth, but he pushed her hand away and flopped his head against her chest. He wouldn't drink any water from a cup either, but spluttered and coughed it out. "Maybe you are just tired," she said. "Maybe we will try again tomorrow." She lifted Kitwana and placed him down in the bed of leaves and hoped that she was right. She blew out the lamp, lay down next to the crate, and fell into an uneasy, broken sleep, worrying that Kitwana would not wake to see the dawn.

Imara woke to the pattering of rain on the hut roof and morning light slicing through the gaps in the wall. She sat up and inhaled deeply. Rain had fallen in the night. It ran in rivulets of red mud across Imara's floor. Her clothes were cold and damp and her sleeping blankets were soaked. She hardly dared look across to Kitwana in his crate. When she did, he looked so still. She tried to see if his chest rose and fell, but she couldn't see any movement at all. She reached out to touch him. His fur was wet through to his skin where water had leaked into the crate, and the palms of his hands and feet were cold and clammy. Imara placed her hand on his chest and beneath her fingers she could feel the flutter of a heartbeat. Relief flooded through her. She sat up and hauled Kitwana into her lap, wrapping her arms around him. His eyes half opened and looked back at her.

"I'll find you food today," she promised, stroking his head. She curled her hand in his, but his hand was too weak to grip hers.

Imara pushed open the door to her hut and looked out. Saka had already lit the fire and put water on to boil and Frog was stoking the fire with more charcoal.

"Saka!" she called. She walked across to him, holding Kitwana's limp body close against her. "Kitwana needs food from the forest. Come with me and find what he will eat."

Frog stopped to look down at the small gorilla. He reached out to touch its hand. "Wait! He is too cold." Frog slipped away and returned with his own threadbare blanket. "Here," he said, placing it around Imara's shoulders and Kitwana. "You are cold, too."

Imara flinched at his kindness.

Don't let him in, warned the demon. **He is the weak one. Don't show him mercy.**

Frog looked across at Imara's hut, at the water streaming through its center. He picked up his shovel. "I will make sure you both stay dry and warm at night."

Imara watched him lumber over to her hut, where he began to dig into the earth.

She followed him. "What are you doing?"

Frog continued to dig two deep channels around the hut. "I need to stop water coming through your hut. See, now the water will flow around it. Now you will be dry."

He wants something from you, Imara. Don't trust him. Ask him what he wants. Why's he helping us?

"Why?" Imara narrowed her eyes. "Why are you doing this?"

Frog leaned on his shovel. Imara could see he had lost weight despite Saka's food parcels.

Don't trust him, Imara.

"Why?" she demanded.

Frog shrugged his shoulders.

He's using you.

Imara pushed the boy's head up with her hand. "Why do this for me? What do you want in return?"

"Nothing," said Frog.

"Nothing?" Imara took a step back and glanced back at Saka. "I see you two together all the time. Why do you look out for each other? What business have you got with a pygmy boy? He is not your kin. Don't you hate him?"

Frog turned away and dug his shovel hard into the earth. "I don't hate anyone."

Imara stared at him and lowered her voice. "Not even the Mambas?"

Frog shook his head.

Imara leaned forward. "But the Mambas took you

from your family," she whispered. "They destroyed everything. Don't you hate them for that?"

Frog stopped digging and turned. He took Kitwana's small hand in his. "Mama told me if you let hate in, it eats your soul. It leaves you empty. Hollowed out, with nothing left but hate inside. I promised her that whatever happened, I'd *never* let it in."

Imara scowled at Frog and walked away, snapping her fingers for Saka to follow. Frog unsettled her in a way she couldn't understand . . . a way she didn't want to understand. She walked with Saka deeper and deeper into the forest, hacking at the vines and grasses. Saka walked ahead of her, plucking leaves and stopping to offer Kitwana different foods. He tried feeding wild celery and nettles, but Kitwana wouldn't eat anything at all. He turned away, pressing his head into Imara's chest.

Imara flicked the uneaten nettles on the ground. "Maybe gorillas don't eat this stuff."

"They do," insisted Saka. "It is one of their favorites."

"How do *you* know?" she said, narrowing her eyes.

Saka paused as if he was deciding whether or not to talk. "I am Batwa," he said quietly. "I belong to the forest."

Careful, whispered the demon. **You are letting Saka and Frog too close. You are letting them tell you their stories.**

"So why won't Kitwana eat?" snapped Imara.

Saka shrugged his shoulders. "Maybe he is homesick. Maybe he belongs with his family in the forest too."

Imara looked across at Saka, but he had turned his back to her.

The demon clamped his fist around her heart. **Remember, he is no friend of yours.**

"Kitwana will eat when he is hungry enough," said Imara, turning to head back to camp. She tried to sound more confident than she felt. Maybe she would try to feed more rice and banana, but she wondered just how long the gorilla would survive.

Saka checked on his snares as they walked back to camp. He bent down to inspect the nooses, frowning as he did so. "Empty again. The game has moved farther into the forest. I will need to set traps deeper in."

Imara pushed ahead of him and walked back into the camp along the lower edge of the coltan mine. Every day, more men arrived to dig the ground, burrowing deep trenches in search of the gray rock they hoped would make them rich. Imara watched them swinging their shovels and picks into the ground, breaking up the red earth and washing and sieving the rocks in the streambed. Some days the sweat glistened from their backs as they worked beneath the hot sun, and other days the miners worked in the rain, their bodies turning dark red with mud. Every day the forest retreated from the mine, as the trees were cut for timber and firewood. The charcoal kilns puffed constant thick smoke into the air, which hung like dirty clouds in the canopy of leaves.

Imara could see Frog working back in the mine. Many of the other miners were older men, their faces leathered by the sun. There were nearly fifty men on Bundi's books. Some came with wives and families in tow, setting up camp on the far side of the river. The children scratched and scraped for coltan in the mine too.

The Black Mamba's men didn't mine the ground. They became the guards. They patrolled the mine, and made sure no one took coltan out into the forest. No one dared. If they did, they knew they would be shot. The Mambas grew lazy on dagga and beer. They liked to sleep late into the day and give out fines to miners who did not dig fast enough or for long enough.

As Imara walked back into camp, she could see some Mambas gathered beside the Black Mamba's hut. They looked excited, jabbing their guns into the air and hooting like chimpanzees that had cornered their prey.

Imara tried to catch glimpses of their prize. Had

they found another gorilla? If they had, what would happen to Kitwana?

Imara tried to squeeze her way through the tight circle of men.

But it was not a gorilla the Mambas had caught. It was a boy.

CHAPTER EIGHTEEN

imara

R at pushed the boy to the ground. "We found him coming here on the miners' track through the forest."

The Black Mamba put his hands behind his back and walked up and down. "How old are you?"

"Sixteen," the boy lied.

Imara craned her neck to see him. The boy was tall but didn't look sixteen. His clothes were muddied and stained with sweat but they weren't worn and threadbare like the other children's clothes. This boy wore shoes, too.

The Black Mamba stared into the boy's eyes. "Why are you in the forests?"

"I came to mine for coltan," said the boy.

"Without a shovel?" said the Black Mamba.

Rat smirked beside him.

Imara edged closer.

The Black Mamba held up the boy's hands. He threw back his head and laughed. "These are soft hands . . . a girl's hands."

Rat laughed and jabbed the boy in the back with his rifle.

The Black Mamba leaned forward. "I do not think these hands have done a day's hard work."

"A spy," spat Rat.

The boy lifted his head up high. "My mother and father are dead. I have come to work," he said.

The Black Mamba glanced at Imara. "Imara," he called. "Come. Meet this new recruit."

Imara pulled the blanket around Kitwana, hiding him from view, and slid out from the crowd. She stood in front of the boy and stared at him.

The boy turned to look at her, taking in the long scar on her face, before he looked away.

The Black Mamba laughed again. "I see you have heard of our Spirit Child. You will not look her in the eye."

Imara watched the boy. Behind his soft eyes there was something else about him. A dangerous stillness. A silence.

"Imara," said the Black Mamba, "this boy says he is looking for work. He says his mother and father are dead. Does he speak the truth?"

The demon whispered in her ear. **He lies. Look, he is young and strong, not broken like the other men. He comes to fight.**

"Well, Imara, does he speak the truth?"

"He lies," said Imara.

Rat pushed the end of his rifle in the boy's back. "I told you . . . a government spy."

The Black Mamba pushed his face nearer the boy. "Why has he come here?"

Imara looked at the boy. His face was expressionless, although the muscles of his jaw were clenched tight. "He comes to fight," she said.

The Black Mamba's lips curled up in a smile. "So, you want to be a Mamba?"

The boy nodded.

The Black Mamba pushed his face even closer. "You think you can just walk in here and we just take you in?"

The other Mambas smirked.

The Black Mamba pulled back his sleeve to show a long snake-shaped scar on his forearm. "You need to earn a place among us. What makes you think you have what it takes to become a Mamba?"

The boy looked at Imara, staring deep into her eyes. "I can look death in the face," said the boy. "I am not afraid to die."

Don't trust him, Imara. This one is different. He is angry. This one is fighting a different battle.

The Black Mamba stepped back. "Brave words, but words are not enough. We will put him in the mines and see what he is made of. Let us see if he is strong enough to become one of us."

Kitwana shifted in Imara's arms, pulling a corner of the blanket from his face. The boy's eyes fixed on the young gorilla. Imara could see his mask of hardness slip for a fleeting moment. It was a moment of recognition. A moment he tried to hide, turning his face away. But Imara had seen it.

The Black Mamba had seen it too. "You are interested in the gorilla!"

It was a statement, not a question.

The boy glanced at the gorilla. He shrugged his shoulders. "I have not seen one before."

"He lies," said Imara.

The Black Mamba leaned closer. "What is your business with gorillas, boy?"

Rat moved closer and leveled his gun. "A spy, a ranger . . . it is all the same to us."

"My father . . . ," began the boy, "my father traded gorillas and chimpanzees before he died. He smuggled them across the border for money. Big money."

He lies he lies he lies.

The Black Mamba narrowed his eyes. Imara could see he didn't believe the boy's story either.

Rat released the safety catch of his rifle and held the rifle to the boy's chest.

The boy swallowed hard, fighting for time. "This gorilla is sick," he said. "It will die unless you know how to look after it. I know how. I had to feed them for my father and keep them alive for the clients."

The Black Mamba pushed Rat's gun away. He lifted the gorilla's limp arm and dropped it to show how weak it was. "So, gorilla boy, what does this one need?"

"Milk," said the boy. "It is a young one, maybe a year old. It was still feeding from its mother."

"And where do we find milk?" said the Black Mamba.

The boy looked around. "Do you have a goat?"

"We ate it," sneered Rat.

"You need powdered milk, the sort you get for human babies. And a bottle," said the boy.

Rat laughed. "If you hadn't noticed, this is the jungle."

The Black Mamba studied the boy. "Powdered milk will save it?"

The boy nodded.

"Bundi," snapped the Black Mamba, "radio the bluebird. Say we need powdered milk and a bottle with the rest of the goods tomorrow. Tell the pilot not to bother to come at all unless he has what I have asked for." He turned to the boy. "If the gorilla dies, you die."

Imara didn't take her eyes from the boy. The evening was cooling, but sweat trickled down his face. His nostrils flared with breathing he was trying to control. "What is your name?" She looked deep into his eyes. "What is your *real* name?"

The boy looked back at her. "Bobo," he said.

He tells the truth.

The boy cleared his throat. "My name is Boboto."

CHAPTER NINETEEN

bobo

My name is Boboto."

Bobo could hear his own voice saying his name, but it seemed detached from him somehow, as if someone else was doing the talking. Everything felt unreal and yet more real and vivid than anything he had felt before. His life hung on the precarious edge of being, or not being, and for one brief moment he had looked into the void. Beads of sweat formed on his forehead and ran down the creases of his nose. He could taste the saltiness on his lips. He clenched his fists and tried to stop his legs from shaking. The Black Mamba was standing right in front of him.

Bobo knew he couldn't hide his fear. The Black Mamba had not been fooled by his story, but he wanted the young gorilla to stay alive and this alone had saved Bobo's life, so far. The young gorilla was Hisani's son, he was sure of it. He could tell by the wide flat noseprint he had come to know. Kambale had said Hodari, the silverback, was dead, but what of the rest of the group? Where were they now? And where was Papa?

Now Bobo was trapped in the rebel camp with no plan at all. The idea that he could walk into the Black Mamba's camp and demand to see his father seemed a childish fantasy now. This was the real world, a world of men.

Only two nights ago he had left his mother and hitched a lift on a logging truck heading along the highway through the forest. He had stopped at one of the trading posts to find out about the coltan mine. Two men drinking beer had just returned from the mine and pointed in the direction of the camp, and Bobo had followed the track into the forest, a path worn and muddied by many feet. The camp wasn't hard to find, but the Mambas guarding the checkpoints hadn't believed his story.

On the way, he had built a fantasy in his head that he would find his father and escape with him into the forest. But now he didn't know what to do. Yet, the gorilla baby was here in the Spirit Child's arms. Maybe his father was here, imprisoned somewhere. Maybe he was hiding in the forest planning to rescue the gorilla. Maybe his father was watching him right now.

"Boboto," said the Spirit Child. "Kitwana needs something to eat until the milk arrives. What will he eat?"

"Kitwana?" said Bobo. "Is that his name?"

The Spirit Child frowned and watched him carefully. "You sound as if he has another one."

Bobo shuffled his feet and looked at Imara, at the long raised scar that split her face in two. After all the stories, he'd expected to be terrified of her, but here she looked like just a girl, her arms wrapped around the gorilla as she might cradle a baby brother.

Bobo turned and pointed through the trees. "We need to go into the forest to find his food."

Rat laughed. "So you can try to escape?"

Bobo shook his head. "The gorilla needs forest food. It is the only way."

"Then bind Bobo's hands," said the Black Mamba. He nodded to Rat. "Go with them into the forest. If he tries to run, shoot him dead."

Bobo walked between Imara and Rat along the forest paths. Rat walked at the back, swinging his gun around his shoulders, as if he was hoping for an excuse to use it. The ropes cut deep into Bobo's wrists and he tried to concentrate on not falling over the tree roots and lianas that snaked across the ground. As they walked farther into the forest, the sounds of the mine and the camp faded. Bobo looked for signs of gorillas or elephants, but there were none. The forest was strangely still and silent. No birdsong, no glimpses of black-and-white colobus monkeys leaping through the trees.

"Stop here," said Bobo as they reached a clearing. "See, there are plenty of young nettles."

Imara scowled. "We have tried those already. He will not eat."

"He *will* eat them," said Bobo.

Imara snatched at the young nettles, wincing as the tiny hairs stung the palms of her hands. She unwrapped the towel to show Kitwana and pushed the nettles near his mouth. "See! He won't eat." Kitwana lay limp in her arms, his eyes half closed. She pushed the gorilla toward Bobo. "He is too sick," she said. "What does he need?"

Bobo stared down into Kitwana's face. He looked so different from the lively gorilla he had known, the one who tried to take the rangers' notebooks and liked to annoy Enzi, the blackback. He thought of his father's last photo of Kitwana clinging to his mother, warmed by her body and sheltered from the rain.

"He needs his mother," said Bobo. "But she is not here. You need to show him what to do."

Imara looked up at Bobo. "How?"

Bobo was aware of Rat, sitting with his gun on his legs, silently watching.

"You need to show him what to eat and *how* to eat," said Bobo. "His mother would have picked the nettles and folded them in her hands, making sure all the stinging hairs are pointing inward."

Imara followed Bobo's instructions, folding the stinging leaves into a ball in her hands.

"Now you must pretend to chew," said Bobo. "You must show what is safe to eat."

Imara nibbled on the ball of nettles, and as she chewed, Kitwana watched her, blinking intently. The leaves were bitter, but not unpleasant. Kitwana reached out his fingers to touch the green juices dribbling down her chin.

"Offer some to him," said Bobo. "He is ready."

Imara offered the ball of nettles to Kitwana. He took them and held them close to his mouth, poking out his tongue and tasting the green juices, playing with the leaves in his hands.

"He is still not eating," said Imara.

"Go slowly," whispered Bobo, sitting down next to her. "This will take time. Even if it takes all day."

Imara chewed the nettles too, and as she did, Kitwana put some in his mouth and rolled the leaves around his tongue.

Bobo watched them both. He watched Kitwana look up into Imara's eyes. "He needs you to look after him."

Imara looked up and frowned.

"He needs you," repeated Bobo. "You must be the one to protect him, to hold him close to you and curl up with at night. If he is to live, you must become his world. You are his mother now."

imara

Imara lay down on her sleeping mat with Kitwana beside her that night. She covered him with her blanket and curled her body around him, feeling him warm up against her skin. She lay awake, breathing in the musty sweet smell of him, outlining his shape in the darkness. He snuffled and wriggled in his sleep. His small hands and feet pulled himself closer to her, gripping her clothes, holding on to her, as if he wouldn't let her go.

Imara could feel more strength in his fingers. Bobo, the new boy with the soft eyes and the silence, had saved him. The demon stirred restlessly at the thought of him and turned somersaults, trying to push him out of Imara's mind. But it wasn't the demon's voice she heard, it was Bobo's. *Kitwana needs you. You are his world. You are his mother now.*

As Imara fell into sleep, the woman with the coffee-colored skin walked through her dreams. She could almost feel the woman's fingertips brush her forehead.

Imara smiled. "Kitwana is safe now," she murmured, holding him close. "He is safe, with me."

The bluebird came clattering out of the sky in the morning. Imara was expecting the White Lioness to be on board, but there was only the pilot. She watched as the Black Mamba's weapons were carried out and laid on pallets, while Bundi counted the boxes of bullets and new guns. The Mambas unloaded more sacks of rice, crates of beer, tinned meat and fish, coffee, tea, and a drum of oil for the generator. Bundi ticked everything off in his book and then signaled for the sacks of coltan to be carried into the helicopter.

Imara walked over to Bundi, Kitwana resting on her hip. Kitwana seemed brighter, but his eyes looked sunken and his stomach was still hollow. "Where is the milk powder for Kitwana? The Black Mamba ordered it yesterday."

Bundi checked through the list and called in through the pilot's door; the pilot reached beneath his seat and pulled out a small package. Bundi tipped out the contents and passed a white plastic box and a bottle to Imara. She took them, sliding them beneath her blanket, and walked back with Kitwana to her hut.

Inside, she put Kitwana on the floor and gave him a piece of wild celery to chew. She opened the plastic box to find white powder inside. She dipped her finger in and licked it, tasting the sweet creaminess of the magic powder that would keep Kitwana alive. She closed the lid and turned the box over and over, tracing her fingers across the instructions, printed words she couldn't read.

She had no choice. She would have to find Bobo to help her.

Saka was sitting near the fire, skinning a wild bush-pig caught in a snare from the night before.

"Where is Bobo?" she said. "I need him now."

Saka stood up. "He's in the mines. Come," he said, "I'll help you find him." He glanced at Kitwana in her arms. "He looks better."

Don't talk to him.

"Just take me to Bobo," said Imara, following Saka around the high rim of the mine.

"There," said Saka. He pointed down in the ravine where Bobo was working a section of the mine with Frog.

Rat was leaning back against the red mud, a cigarette hanging from the corner of his mouth, his arm casually resting on his gun. He was watching Bobo shovel spade after spade of red earth into a bucket. Bobo's shoulders glistened with sweat, and Imara could see the strain in his muscles. Frog's job was to wash the shoveled earth and separate the mud from the lumps of coltan. Imara noticed Frog had lost more weight. His hands shook as he tried to lift another bucket. He didn't look as if he could go on much more. His knees buckled under the weight and he sank down, sliding on the mud.

Rat kicked him. "Get up, get up."

Frog tried but floundered in the mud. Rat kicked him hard in the stomach. "Get up. GET. UP."

Saka gripped Imara's arm. "He'll kill him."

Imara shook Saka off, but watched as Bobo turned and advanced on Rat, his shovel raised above his head.

Rat scrambled backward, grabbed his gun, and leveled it at Bobo.

"Stop!" shouted Imara.

Both Rat and Bobo looked up at her.

"I need him," said Imara, pointing at Bobo. She looked at Frog doubled over in the mud. She knew Rat would kick him again once Bobo had left. "And I need Frog, too," she called. "I need him to fetch me water."

What are you doing? hissed the demon. **Frog is not your business. Don't show him mercy. Rat will tell the Black Mamba of your weakness.**

"You don't need both of them!" shouted Rat.

See . . . See what will happen . . . Rat will do anything to bring you down. I am the only one who can protect you.

Imara glared down at Rat. "Do you challenge me?"

Rat turned his face away, kicking at the mud.

"Send them both up to me," ordered Imara. "I need them now."

Imara walked behind Bobo and Saka, watching them carry Frog between them.

They are nothing to you, Imara. Nothing. Don't pity them.

Back at the camp, Imara pointed at Frog. "He is too sick to work. Saka, take him away. Let him sleep."

Frog stumbled forward. "Thank you," he said.

Imara spat on the floor beside him. "Don't thank me. You are no use to me dead."

She watched them go and then turned to Bobo, handing him the box of powdered milk. "What do I do with this?"

Bobo took the milk powder from her hands and looked on both sides of the box. His eyes scanned the words.

"You can read?" said Imara.

Bobo nodded.

"You've been to school?"

Bobo frowned. "My father taught me," he said.

Imara saw a shield come across his eyes. So he had secrets, too.

Bobo pulled out a small plastic scoop. "We need to mix the powder with warm water that's already been boiled."

"There's some in the pot," said Imara. She reached in with her finger. "It's warm still."

Imara watched Bobo measure out the powder and scoop it into the bottle. He added the water and shook the bottle, the water becoming white as it mixed with the powder.

"Here," he said. "See if he takes some."

Imara tried to push the teat into Kitwana's mouth, but he pushed it away, closing his lips tight shut. "What now?"

"You have to be a gorilla," said Bobo. "You have to talk his language."

Imara could see the corner of his mouth curl up in a smile. She scowled. "Don't make fun of me."

Bobo laughed. "I mean it. When you give the milk you must make him calm. Gorillas grunt softly when they are content." He gave a low grunting sound that sounded more like a belch. "Talk to him. Let him taste the milk first, too. You must show him there is nothing to worry about."

Imara tried grunting, but Kitwana pushed her away.

Bobo took the bottle. "You hold him. I'll try to get him to take the milk." Bobo leaned forward, so his face was close to Kitwana. He grunted deep in his chest. The gorilla's eyes found Bobo's and stared into them in mild surprise. Bobo let a drop of milk fall into Kitwana's mouth. The young gorilla tasted it, rolling the liquid around his tongue. His lips reached forward for another taste. Bobo let another drop fall.

"There," said Bobo. He let Kitwana take the end of the bottle in his mouth. Kitwana chewed on the end, then his small eyes lit up as he found how to suck the warm milk into his mouth.

"See," said Bobo, smiling. He handed the bottle to Imara. "Now you do it."

Imara held the bottle and looked down into Kitwana's eyes staring up at her. She held the bottle to his mouth. "Am I doing it right?"

"He looks like he's enjoying it to me," said Bobo.

Kitwana kept sucking the bottle long after it was empty. He held it in his hands, refusing to let it go. Imara couldn't help smiling at him. She scratched his tummy and he curled his legs up in delight.

She heard Bobo laugh and looked up.

Bobo nudged her. "Aha . . . and so you *can* smile after all."

Don't smile. He is not your friend.

Imara frowned and glared at Bobo. She could feel the tightness of her scar. "Don't forget who I am."

Bobo pulled a piece of vine and twisted it in his fingers. "What makes you the Black Mamba's Spirit Child?"

"Are you challenging me?"

"No, just asking," said Bobo.

Imara thrust the palm of her right hand near Bobo's face. "This," she said, showing him two dark purple marks on her palm near her thumb. "This is what makes me a Spirit Child. I was bitten by a black mamba and survived. The Black Mamba says powerful spirits protect me."

Bobo stared at the snakebite and smiled. He shook his head and chuckled to himself.

"What's so funny?" snapped Imara.

"You were just lucky," he whispered.

"Lucky?" frowned Imara. "No one survives a black mamba bite."

"They do if it's a dry bite," said Bobo. "A snake

can bite without injecting venom. My father knew a man it happened to."

The demon recoiled inside her. **No! No one must know!**

Imara clenched her hand and held it against her chest. "You tell lies," she blurted out. "I'm the Black Mamba's Spirit Child."

Bobo moved around to sit next to her. "I won't tell," he whispered.

Be careful, Imara. Don't tell him anything about you.

Imara pulled the bottle from Kitwana's grip and lifted him up against her chest. The warm milk had revived him, and he started pulling at a button on her shirt. He pulled it off and pushed his finger through the buttonhole.

She felt Bobo still watching her and looked up.

Bobo nodded toward the camp. "How long have you been with the Mambas?"

Imara shrugged. "Long enough."

"Where are you from?" he said softly.

Imara glared at him. Out of the corner of her eye she could see Rat looking their way.

You fool, Imara. You're letting Bobo get too close. Rat has already seen.

"Who are you?" persisted Bobo. "Where is your family?"

Rat is watching you.

Imara stood up. "I have no family," she said, folding her face into a scowl.

Bobo leaned forward. "You must have. You are someone's daughter, someone's child," he whispered.

"I am the devil's child," spat Imara.

Rat sauntered over to them, his boots slapping in the wet mud. He looked from Bobo to Imara. "Black Mamba," he called. "We have a problem."

The Black Mamba looked across at them. "What is it?"

Rat shoved the end of his rifle into Bobo's chest. "It seems Bobo is fond of your Spirit Child."

The Black Mamba walked over and stared down at Imara.

"Kitwana is getting better," she said, trying to deflect Rat's accusations. "See, the milk is making him strong. Bobo has helped to save him."

Rat glanced sideways at Imara. "I wonder whose side Bobo is on?"

The Black Mamba slung his gun across his shoulder. "There is a village causing us some trouble not far from here. Tomorrow I will take some men with me to go and see the chief. Let the new boy come with us. Then we can see where his loyalties really lie."

imara

Imara put her eye to one of the gaps in her hut and watched the Black Mamba and his men gather around the fire. Kitwana tugged at her shorts, wanting to be picked up. He had drunk three bottles of milk since the morning and already he was stronger. His skin had filled out and didn't look papery thin anymore. His eyes were bright and curious and he had begun to explore Imara's hut, pulling at the spare clothes she kept tied up from the low roof. Imara shifted position to get a better view of the fire. She tried to look for Bobo but couldn't see him.

Darkness was approaching, brought early by the heavy clouds. A wind blew restlessly in the canopy of leaves. Rat handed out guns and ammunition to the chosen men. Dikembe stood behind them, a panga in his hand, staring at the ground.

Imara picked up Kitwana and hugged him to her. The Black Mamba was planning a dawn raid. She was glad she wouldn't see this raid. She had heard the Black Mamba talk of a village on the edge of the park. The villagers had complained about the mine destroying the park and about the rebels who stole their livestock and threatened their people. The Black Mamba wanted to talk with their chief. Imara scanned the assortment of weapons in the Mambas' hands, knowing the Kalashnikovs and pangas would be doing the talking.

Imara looked again for Bobo in the group. Maybe he wouldn't join this raid. But then she saw him. The Black Mamba called him forward and handed him a panga. She knew that new recruits had to earn a gun. She watched Bobo staring at the panga, turning it over and over in his hand. He would have to prove himself or die.

"Imara!" The Black Mamba called her name. "Come and protect the men."

Kitwana clung to Imara as she walked across to the fire. She scooped ash into an earthen bowl and mixed it with water into a paste. The men lined up in front of her to have the ash snake painted on their skin.

Kitwana sat and watched, dipping his finger into the bowl of ash and tasting it, pulling faces at the gritty texture in his mouth.

Only Bobo didn't come forward. Imara walked up to him with her bowl of wet ash. She held his wrist. "Let me protect you too."

Bobo pulled his arm away. "Protect me from what?"

"From harm."

Bobo took a step back from her.

Imara could see his breaths were sharp and shallow. He shook his head and walked away from her to join the other Mambas.

Come away, whispered the demon. **Don't look. He is nothing to you.**

But Imara couldn't help looking. She wished that she could protect him. She watched him clenching and unclenching his fists. She noticed he didn't take a swig of beer or a wad of dagga when the Black Mamba passed them around.

Come away, Imara. It is best that he dies. If he does come back, he will not be the same boy he is now.

Imara tried to hold the image of him, the boy with the soft eyes and silence. It was how she wanted to remember him. She turned away and walked back to the darkness of her hut with Kitwana, shutting the door behind her. The demon wrapped his arms around her.

Keep me in here, Imara. Just you and me. Together we are strong. Together, we don't need anyone at all.

The camp was quiet after the Black Mamba and his men had left. The remaining Mambas relaxed, and passed around more beer. Two guarded the Black Mamba's hut where the weapons and mined coltan were stored. A dim yellow light glowed from the hut, and Imara could imagine Bundi in there, hunched over his books, meticulously filling in his forms.

Rain started to fall, the drops pattering softly through leaves and bouncing off the tarpaulin roof of Imara's hut. She was warm and dry. She curled herself up in her blanket and listened to the slow steady breathing of Kitwana, in time with hers.

She was falling asleep when she heard a soft knock at her door.

Imara edged closer to the door and peered out through the crack. "Saka, what are you doing here?" she whispered.

"Frog is sick," he said. "I can't wake him. He is muttering to the spirits."

Imara opened the door a little wider. "What do you want?"

"Can you ask the spirits to make him better?"

"It is up to them to decide," said Imara coldly.

Saka pushed his way through the door. "I think he will die."

Tell him to go away. Tell him death is a blessing in this place.

"Go away," said Imara.

Saka held on to Imara's arm. "Please, Imara. Please help him."

Imara looked at Saka, and then beyond him to the Black Mamba's men huddled around the fire. She nodded, glancing back at Kitwana to check that he was still sleeping. "Take me to Frog," she said. "And quietly. No one must see."

Imara followed Saka, keeping in the shadows, out of sight of the men. She crawled beneath the tarpaulin shelter he and Frog shared. Saka switched on a small flashlight.

"Where did you get that flashlight?" she said.

"I found it," he said.

"Where?"

"It doesn't matter," he said, pointing it at Frog.

In the flickering light of the yellow bulb, Imara could see that Saka had tried to keep Frog dry with some of the sacks for coltan. He'd managed to find extra blankets for him too, but Frog had thrown them off and was lying in the mud, his whole body shaking.

Imara bent down beside Frog. She wrinkled her nose. Frog had the sickness and diarrhea. His clothes and body stank with it.

Frog grabbed her arm, his eyes wide. His teeth chattered as he tried to talk. "It's all true of course . . . every word."

Imara glanced at Saka. "What's he talking about?"

"A story," said Saka. "He keeps telling a story of the lion and the mamba, telling it over and over."

"A story," said Imara. "Stories won't save him now."

Frog fell into a fevered giggle. "When they fight, who wins the battle?"

Imara felt Frog's forehead with her hand. "The lion," she said. "He kills the snake."

Frog shook his head wildly from side to side. "They both die. The mamba dies quickly in the lion's mouth, but not before he's bitten the lion with venom. The lion dies . . . death is slow and painful."

Imara watched Frog yabbering his thoughts into the air. Sweat poured from him, soaking into his clothes. "When did he eat last?"

"Two days ago," said Saka.

"He needs food and water," she said.

Saka clutched her arm. "He needs medicine too."

"Wait here," said Imara, slipping out into the night. She kept a wide circle around the Mambas and crept into her hut. Kitwana had wriggled in his sleep, his arm curled around Imara's blanket for comfort. Imara reached up for the sachets of medicine hidden between the sheets of tarpaulin.

What are you doing? You might need this medicine for yourself.

Frog kept my hut dry, she argued with the demon. *He helped Kitwana, and he helped me too.*

You owe him nothing. If you get sick you will

die instead, weak and lying in your own mess.

Imara snatched the two sachets and left the hut before the demon could change her mind. She crouched down beside Saka. "I have two sachets of medicine left. Frog can have them, but it is all I have."

"Thank you," said Saka, staring at the sachets.

"You need to mix them with water. Go fetch some and I will help him drink."

Imara waited in the shelter for Saka to fetch water, trying to ignore the demon yelling in her ear.

Stupid girl. You are risking everything. Everything!

"Help me up with him," Imara said on Saka's return. She mixed one sachet in a cup of water. "He must drink."

Saka helped Frog to sit up and Imara put the medicine to his lips and watched him take small sips.

Frog turned to her, blinking in the darkness. "Mama?"

"I am not your mama," snapped Imara. "Now drink. It will make you better."

When Imara had finished, she gave the last sachet to Saka. "Here. Give him this in the night. Do not let anyone see. If they find it on you, I will say you have stolen it. Do you understand?"

Saka took the sachet. "Thank you."

"Don't ask anything of me again." Imara crawled out of the shelter and made her way back to her hut through the shadows with the demon fuming inside her. **Imara, you are becoming weak. What are you doing? You should have kept the medicine for yourself.**

Imara woke before dawn. She tried to push the thought of Bobo from her head. She knew the Black Mamba's ways. She knew they would be lining up along the forest edge, waiting to attack. The Mambas were like the forest ants. They destroyed and devoured anything in their way. Imara imagined Bobo with his panga at his side, running into battle. If he didn't join in the fight, the Mambas would kill him anyway. She hoped he would escape and leave, but Bobo had some other battle and Imara knew he wouldn't leave until it had been fought.

She tried to keep herself busy, giving Kitwana his milk and collecting plants from the forest for him to eat. Frog looked better. She saw him sitting up, scraping out a bowl of rice. Saka tried to catch Imara's eye, but she ignored him. She didn't want the Mambas to think she was any friend of Saka or Frog.

It wasn't until the late afternoon that the Black Mamba and his men returned, their arrival announced by the crackle of the radio and the sudden busyness of the Mambas guarding the camp.

The men returned high on adrenaline and beer, laughing and shouting, firing shots into the sky. They carried goats and bags filled with chickens, which they released into the camp. The chickens clucked and scurried in a flurry of feathers across the ground. All the Mambas had returned, all except the boy, Dikembe, but no one spoke about him as if he was forgotten already. The Black Mamba was happy. He drank his beer, holding the wrist of a young woman at his side. He had found himself a new wife. It had been another good raid.

Imara searched the crowd of men for Bobo. Then she saw him standing, shoulders slumped, his arms loose at his sides. The boy she knew had returned, but in his face she saw an emptiness. A haunting. The Black Mamba pushed Bobo forward into the firelight. He took his arm and held it up high. "We have a new Mamba," he shouted. "Bobo is one of us now."

The men cheered, holding their beer bottles high in the air. Only Rat threw sidelong glances at Bobo, from his small suspicious eyes. He bit the cap off a beer bottle and spat it on the ground.

The Black Mamba was smiling. He picked up a Kalashnikov rifle and thrust it into Bobo's hand. "Today you became a man."

The Black Mamba pushed a beer into Bobo's other hand, and Imara watched Bobo drink it, not stopping until the bottle was empty. When Bobo finished, he just stared ahead, his face blank. Expressionless. Imara had seen new recruits look like it before. It was never easy, the first raid. She had seen it too many times.

It was always the same.

The gun made men of boys, and monsters of men.

Imara waited and watched as the Mambas drank and shared their stories, each story becoming more embellished with bravado as the beer took hold. She saw Bobo slide away into the forest. She chose her moment and slipped out of her hut, with Kitwana clinging to her, and followed him along the trails until she saw him crouched by the riverbed. He was kneeling in the water, bent over, scrubbing his arms with his nails. She could see the raw raised marks where his fingernails had scratched his skin.

"Bobo," she said.

Bobo spun around, staring as if he had never seen her before.

"It's me. Me and Kitwana."

Bobo glanced at them and then turned back to scrubbing his arms.

"The Black Mamba is pleased with you today," she said. "He says you are a Mamba now."

Bobo stopped scrubbing. He sat down on a rock and stared into the water. "Today, I watched an innocent man die, and I did nothing to save him." said Bobo. "Nothing."

Imara could see his hands shaking. "You couldn't do anything," she said, kneeling down beside him. "Or you would have been killed as well."

Bobo washed water over his head as if trying to wash away the memory. "He was protecting his family."

Kitwana clung to Imara and eyed Bobo as if he was a different boy from the one before. "You had no choice," said Imara.

"I *had* a choice," said Bobo. He wrung his hands together. "In that split second I *had* a choice. But I was scared. I chose the wrong one. I could have tried to save a man's life. He was someone's father, someone's husband, someone's son."

Imara shook her head. "And you would both be dead now, if you had tried to defend him."

"And it would have been better than this," said Bobo. "How can I live knowing I did nothing?"

"You are alive," said Imara. "That's what counts. Only the strong survive."

Bobo shook his head. "I am weak," he said. He leaned forward, clutched his stomach, and retched into the river. When he sat back up, Imara could see the softness in his eyes had gone.

"My father was right," said Bobo, wiping vomit from his mouth. "Only a coward needs a gun to make him strong."

gorilla

Kitwana clung to Imara, curling his fingers into the Girl Ape's clothes. He didn't like these Tall Apes. He wanted his mother and the rest of his family. He wanted to smell them, to hear them and touch them, but in his mind he heard them screaming and saw Hodari lying dead.

Fire-stick blood dead.

Eyes wide, staring.

These Tall Apes were Killer Apes.

They were all young males. Angry, scared, and wary. They had no mothers to protect them or reprimand them. They didn't let each other close. Each one had a boundary *that another couldn't cross. The only thing that bound them together was their fear.*

Kitwana watched them from the safety of the Girl Ape's arms.

The Tall Ape with the snake bones walked with his head high and shoulders back. He barked to the others and they made way for him. No Tall Ape would look him eye to eye. He was the silverback here, but he was not like Hodari. Hodari protected his family, but this Killer Ape needed the other apes to protect him. This Killer Ape cared only for himself. When he turned away, the other Tall Apes squabbled among themselves. Even the small ones had some power. The fire-sticks made the small ones big.

The two youngest Tall Apes were the only ones to cling together. They didn't fear each other. Kitwana had seen them curled next to each other in sleep, like he and Enzi used to do. But the smallest one had been the one to lead other Killer Apes to his family and so Kitwana couldn't trust him.

He trusted the Girl Ape. She was his protection. She kept him safe. He needed to feel her hands holding him. She gave him milk and food and wrapped him in her arms. He slept beside her, warmed by her. Yet, when he closed his eyes, he could see the creased contours of his mother's face, and every time he reached for her, she was running into the dark forest, running and running, away, away.

CHAPTER TWENTY-TWO

imara

The White Lioness arrived the next morning, while Imara was serving mealie porridge for the men. Imara watched her shaking out her mane of golden hair. The Black Mamba was waiting for her, his shirt billowing in the downdraft from the rotor blades. Imara held Kitwana close to her body and felt the demon squirming deep inside, squeezing the breath from her lungs. The White Lioness had come for her prize. She had come for Kitwana.

Imara looked for Bobo among the men. Bobo

hadn't come for food. She could see him sitting by the Black Mamba's hut, his arms wrapped around a gun, staring into space. He had become the Black Mamba's favorite. He was now the Black Mamba's guard.

Rat joined the end of the queue of men lining up for porridge. He waited until he was alone with Imara and then pushed his cup in front of her face. "More," he demanded.

Imara scraped the bottom of the pan and spooned the last of the porridge into his cup. Rat was watching her, a smirk upon his face.

Be careful, whispered the demon. **He comes to taunt you.**

Rat nodded toward Bobo and pulled a sad face. "Your gorilla boy does not love you anymore." He sighed and shook his head. "And soon you will lose your baby, too," he whispered, poking Kitwana in the stomach with his finger. "The White Lioness will take him with her."

Imara drew Kitwana away. She felt the demon

claw at her inside. **Don't say anything. Don't rise to his bait.**

Rat leaned forward. "You don't fool me, Imara. See, I am not afraid to look you in the eye." He stared at her. A triumphant grin stretched across his face. "You have no powers. The Black Mamba will find that out soon enough, and then he will treat you just like any other woman."

Imara closed her eyes and felt bile rise inside her. The demon raged inside. **This is your fault, Imara. You let me out and showed your weakness. I warned you what would happen. I warned you!**

"Imara!"

Imara looked up. The Black Mamba was calling her from his hut, the White Lioness standing beside him.

"Imara, come here."

Rat followed close behind as she made her way across the camp. Kitwana gripped tightly to her, burying his head in her arm. Imara glanced briefly at Bobo, but he didn't even seem to see that she was there.

"So," the White Lioness purred, bending down to look at Kitwana, "the Black Mamba has kept his word."

"See, he is a healthy gorilla," said the Black Mamba.

A frown crossed the White Lioness's face. "I had wanted a girl, but no matter." She ran her fingers through the gorilla's fur. "He will do." She smiled and held her arms out, palms upturned. "Here," she said to Imara. "Let me hold him."

Imara felt the Black Mamba watching. She tried to peel Kitwana away, but he clung to her, gripping with his fingers and toes.

The Black Mamba reached out and pulled Kitwana away from her. "Let the White Lioness hold him," he ordered. Kitwana shrieked, grasping for Imara. A spurt of diarrhea sprayed the Black Mamba's clean shirt. He swore and pushed Kitwana back into Imara's arms.

The White Lioness stepped back and wrinkled her nose. "He is shy," she said. "He is not yet ready for me. But that will change."

The Black Mamba wiped his hands on his shirt. "Rat," he barked. "Get me water to clean myself."

The White Lioness looked amused. She turned to Imara. "The gorilla likes you."

Don't say a word.

Imara stared straight ahead, curling her fingers into Kitwana's fur.

"Well," said the White Lioness, reaching out to stroke his face, "does he have a name?"

Imara gripped Kitwana more tightly and stayed silent.

"The Spirit Child has named him Kitwana," said the Black Mamba.

The White Lioness smiled, not taking her eyes from Imara. "So, the girl is fond of the gorilla too." She studied Imara for a moment. "I almost forgot, I have something for you. I thought a girl in the jungle shouldn't be expected to wear men's clothes."

Imara looked down at her ragged T-shirt and shorts, torn and caked in mud. She felt small and dirty.

"Clarkson," said the White Lioness. "Bring me my bags from the helicopter."

Clarkson returned with a bright bag with soft pink handles.

"Really, Black Mamba," the White Lioness scolded. "You should treat your Spirit Child with more respect." She pulled out a parcel wrapped in tissue paper.

"For you." The White Lioness smiled.

Imara glanced at the Black Mamba and took the package. She felt something soft inside. "What is it?"

"Open it," encouraged the White Lioness.

Imara peeled back the paper, helped by Kitwana who tore it with his fingers, stuffing pink tissue paper in his mouth. The White Lioness laughed, a high nasal laugh, and reached forward to the package, pulling out a red dress printed with white flowers, with a white bow around the waist.

Imara just stared at it.

The White Lioness held the dress next to Imara. "Feel it," she said. "Isn't it beautiful? It's silk."

Imara ran her fingers across the soft ruffles of the dress. It smelled clean and of flowers, not of the forest.

"Put it on." The White Lioness smiled.

Imara tried to put Kitwana on the ground, but he shrieked and didn't stop until the Black Mamba ordered Bobo to hold him. Kitwana quieted in Bobo's arms and chewed the tissue paper, dribbling pink-stained saliva from his lips.

"Go and get changed," said the White Lioness. "I would like to see you in it."

Imara took the dress and walked across the camp. Instead of going to her own hut, she walked a little way through the forest to the stream where she liked to bathe. She took off her shorts and T-shirt and slipped into the water, washing the mud and dirt away, before stepping into the dress. She pulled it over her shoulders and smoothed it over her hips. She leaned over the rocks, trying to catch her reflection in the water. The dress danced in the ripples, bright against the dark water.

It's too good for you, sneered the demon.

Imara put her face closer to a pool of still water to look at her own reflection. She traced her finger down the long raised scar, and scowled.

Look how ugly you are. No one could love you.

She punched the water, shattering her face. She pulled on her boots, grabbed her old clothes from the riverbank, and marched back to the Black Mamba's hut, aware of the other Mambas staring at her.

"Turn around," said the White Lioness.

Imara turned, showing the whole of the dress. The skirt flared out around her.

The White Lioness smiled and looked around the watching Mambas. "A bright flower among the thorns," she said. "Maybe we will make a woman of you yet." She glanced at Imara's worn boots and tutted. "I will bring some pretty shoes next time I come."

Kitwana pulled away from Bobo and clambered into Imara's arms, where he tugged on the bow around her waist.

"Come," said the White Lioness, sitting on the floor of the hut. "Let us play with Kitwana, while Clarkson and the Black Mamba talk business."

Imara sat on the floor with Kitwana. She watched the Black Mamba and Clarkson head out toward the coltan mine. Bobo stood guard at the door, facing out, although his body was angled into the room. Imara could tell he wanted to listen to every word the White Lioness had to say.

The White Lioness opened her handbag and looked inside. "Maybe I will find something for him to play with."

She rolled a small red tube across to Kitwana. Kitwana looked at it before stretching out a finger to poke it. He picked it up in his fingers and pulled two halves of the tube apart and tried to bite one of the halves, crunching the plastic and spitting red blobs onto the ground.

"I don't think he likes lipstick." The White Lioness laughed.

Imara pulled the pieces of plastic from his mouth. "It isn't good for him."

The White Lioness sat back, leaning on her arms, and looked at Imara. "You're very fond of him, aren't you?"

She wants something.

Imara shrugged her shoulders.

The White Lioness tipped her head to one side. "You don't have to leave him," she said.

Imara looked up sharply.

She knows what you want. She has you in her power. Tell her Kitwana means nothing to you.

"There are plenty more gorillas in the forest," said Imara, picking at a knot of wood in the floor. "It makes no difference to me if you take him with you today."

"I'm not taking him today," said the White Lioness. "I'm not ready for him yet."

Imara stared hard at the floor.

You don't fool her, hissed the demon. **She sees what Kitwana means to you.**

The White Lioness leaned forward. "You could come with me," she whispered.

Imara looked up.

A conspiratorial smile slid cross the White Lioness's face. Imara was aware of Bobo, his head tilting ever so slightly toward the inside of the room. Kitwana left Imara's side to sit beside the White Lioness, where he started pulling out the contents of her handbag.

"I could take you away from here," whispered the White Lioness.

Imara tried to reach for Kitwana, but Kitwana grabbed the bag and ran to the corner of the room clutching it to him. He wasn't going to let it go.

"Where would you take us?" asked Imara.

The White Lioness smiled. "To civilization, of course. The Land of Money. There is nothing for you here. I want to help." She took Imara's hand. "I can give you a better life. I can give you anything: pretty dresses, a house to live in, a room of your own. You can be clean again and eat as much food as you want. Kitwana will be safe, too. He will have an enclosure of his own with trees to climb and fruit to eat." She touched Imara's scar. "I know doctors who could take this away. They could make you beautiful again."

Imara frowned and pulled her hand away. "I am the Black Mamba's Spirit Child," she said. "He wouldn't let me go."

The White Lioness laughed. "Everyone has their price, Imara," she said. "Everyone."

Imara turned her head toward the door. She could hear feet on the wet ground outside and the Black Mamba's voice.

"I can take you away from all of this," whispered the White Lioness.

Imara crossed the room and snatched the bag from Kitwana and threw it on the floor next to the White Lioness. She scooped up Kitwana and held his arms to stop him from reaching for the bag again.

"Think about it, and let me know your answer," said the White Lioness. She scratched Kitwana under the chin. "When I come back next week for Kitwana, I can take you with me too."

CHAPTER TWENTY-THREE

imara

This is your chance, Imara. She can take away the scar. No one need ever know I am inside here. She can make you beautiful again.

"Well?" said Bobo.

Imara looked around.

Bobo had followed her to the fire, where she began to heat water to make coffee for the White Lioness.

"Well what?" said Imara, pushing more charcoal into the lazy embers.

"Are you going with her?"

Imara shrugged her shoulders. She glanced across at the Black Mamba's hut where the White Lioness sat, tapping on her phone. "Why not? She can care for Kitwana and me."

"She doesn't want to care for you. She wants to own you," said Bobo, "like she owns all of us, including the Black Mamba."

Imara shook her head. "It's not like that. She wants *us*," she said, glancing across at Kitwana, where he sat rummaging through pots and ladles by the fire.

"She wants power," said Bobo.

Don't listen to him. The White Lioness wants you. She wants to love you. She wants to make you beautiful.

"Kitwana will be safe. We'll have as much food as we can eat. It will be better than here."

"You will not be free," said Bobo.

"What do you know of freedom?" spat Imara.

Bobo stared into the fire. "I know that it isn't this. Look around you. We're no more than slaves while the world steals what's beneath our feet. It's people like us, and the animals, who suffer. Kitwana deserves his freedom. He belongs with his family. He belongs in the forest."

Imara glared at him. "Really? Big words from the boy whose father traded gorillas and chimpanzees!"

"No," said Bobo softly. "My father is not that man."

Imara put one hand on her hip. "Who is he then?"

"My father is a good man."

"Then why doesn't he come to find you?"

Bobo pushed a stick into the fire and stared into the flames. "I don't know," he said. "But if he came, I don't think he would recognize his son."

Imara sat down and stirred the hot water into the ground coffee. She reached for the tin of sugar syrup, but it wasn't where she had left it. She looked up at Bobo. "Someone has taken the syrup tin."

Bobo shrugged his shoulders.

Imara glanced around her. Kitwana had disappeared too. She could feel panic rise inside her. She hadn't noticed him slip away.

She stood up and spun around. "Where's Kitwana?"

Bobo pointed to the log pile and laughed. "There! There is your thief."

Kitwana was sitting on top of the log pile, holding the syrup tin to his mouth, poking his tongue inside.

"Kitwana!" scolded Imara.

Kitwana shrieked on being found out, and held the tin high above his head.

Bobo scrambled up the log pile, but Kitwana threw the tin at him and scuttled down the other side. Bobo looked inside the tin. "At least there's some syrup left." He grinned. "The White Lioness will have her work cut out with Kitwana."

Imara nodded. "But he still needs me. I can't stop her from taking him, and that's why I'll go with her when she takes him next week."

Bobo nodded in the direction of the White

Lioness. "So why is she still here now? Why doesn't she leave?"

"She's waiting," said Imara. She scraped the remaining sugar syrup into the pot.

"For what?"

Imara hooked her fingers through the handles of tin coffee cups and picked up the pot of coffee. "The White Lioness wants official papers to say the Black Mamba is good to his workers and doesn't fund the rebels."

Bobo snorted. "And who will provide that documentation?"

"Him," said Imara. She pointed the spout of the coffee pot toward the forest path where a large man in uniform emerged from the trees, surrounded by bodyguards. He was puffing and panting, holding his sides to catch his breath.

Imara glanced at Bobo. He had stepped back into the shadows, but his eyes were fixed on the man. Imara could see Bobo's teeth clench together, the muscles tightening in his jaw.

He knows him, whispered the demon. **He knows this man. Find out who he is.**

Kitwana crept close to Imara and reached up for her. She crouched down and let him clamber up onto her back, feeling sticky sugar syrup still coating his fingers.

The man stopped to pull out a handkerchief from his pocket and wipe sweat from his forehead.

"He doesn't look like a man who walks in jungles," said Imara.

"He's not," said Bobo, lifting his rifle to his shoulder. "He is used to being driven around in a car."

Imara glanced at Bobo. "Who is he?"

Bobo's face had hardened. "He is Mr. Mutombo, the chief of police."

So this is Bobo's battle. This is why he's here.

"Help me carry the coffee," said Imara. "Let's listen to them talk."

The White Lioness stretched her legs and glanced at the gold watch on her wrist. "You have delayed me," she said to the police chief. "Surely there isn't that much traffic in the jungle?"

The police chief glanced at the Black Mamba. "We could not come as far as we wanted by truck. We have been walking since dawn—"

"Please sit," she interrupted. "I am not interested in your journey here."

Imara walked between them and placed the coffee pot and cups on the low table while Bobo slid into the shadows behind the police chief. Imara served coffee to the Black Mamba, the White Lioness, Clarkson, Bundi, and the police chief, while the police chief's bodyguards paced outside the door, their guns held nervously by their sides.

Clarkson put a small briefcase on the table and opened it, showing dollar notes piled neatly inside. Kitwana climbed down from Imara's arms and edged over to the briefcase, pulling dollars out and stuffing them in his mouth.

The police chief leaned forward to shoo Kitwana away.

"Don't worry," said the White Lioness. "There are plenty more where those came from. But what we need is documentation from you, to say rebels do not control this mine. We need tags for the coltan to say it is from certified mines."

The police chief's eyes flitted between the Black Mamba, the White Lioness, and the briefcase. "It can be done," he said.

The White Lioness offered the police chief a cigarette and held out her lighter for him. "But it seems the mine is within the boundary of the national park. Isn't this a problem?"

The police chief inhaled, lighting the cigarette. He sat back, letting the smoke flow out through his nostrils. "No one needs to know this mine is inside the park. I can provide tags for your coltan to say it is from another mine, one that has been inspected and certified rebel free. No one will know."

The White Lioness raised an eyebrow. "Good," she said. "The companies I deal with like to think they have a clear conscience, even if they don't want to put any effort in to prove it." She sat back and lit her own cigarette. "We also need to get the coltan out of Congo, to Rwanda. I'd rather not have any interference from border controls."

The police chief pulled a fifty-dollar note from the suitcase and rubbed it between his fingers. "I know people on both sides of the border who can make sure your helicopter has safe passage."

"Excellent." The White Lioness smiled. She sat back and looked around, letting her eyes come to rest on Kitwana. "But surely the wildlife rangers will report this mine."

The Black Mamba sipped his coffee. "The police chief has this under control."

"You are a clever man," purred the White Lioness. "Tell me, Mr. Mutombo, how have you done this?"

The police chief nodded and smoothed his trousers, keen to impress the White Lioness. "I have banned ranger patrols in this part of the park due to rebel activity." He smiled to himself and leaned forward. "A ranger was accused of the killing of the silverback. The rangers' authority is tainted. People are scared. You won't get any trouble."

"Good." The White Lioness nodded. "And what if rangers do come here?"

The Black Mamba finished his coffee in a gulp. "Then we do what we have done before. The only good ranger is a dead ranger." He reached for a bag behind stacked tins of food and cooking oil. Imara recognized the bag from the evening when Rat had brought Kitwana into the camp. The Black Mamba emptied the bag, spilling crumpled clothes on the floor. He held up a green jacket. "Let's have our own ranger here in camp." He looked around and threw the jacket to Bobo. "Bobo, you can be our ranger."

Imara could see Bobo's hands shaking as he held the jacket.

The Black Mamba picked a green beret from the floor and spun it across the room. "Put it on, Bobo. Let's see our new ranger."

Bobo caught the beret. He placed the jacket on the floor and turned the beret over and over in his hands. Imara watched him run his fingers around the inside of the rim and push a finger through a hole in the top of the beret. The frayed edges of the material around the hole were fringed with blood. Imara saw the flicker of recognition in Bobo's eyes. It was almost imperceptible, yet she saw it.

In that one moment, Imara knew.

She understood.

She had seen a ghost's shadow pass across Bobo's face.

CHAPTER TWENTY-FOUR

bobo

Bobo turned the beret over, running his fingers across the embroidered name, the name he had seen his mother sew into the rim only two weeks before. It suddenly felt heavy in his hands, as if it carried the weight of the whole forest inside it. Bobo's legs trembled beneath him. The world around him dissolved away; the Black Mamba, the White Lioness, the police chief, Kitwana, the aroma of coffee, and the thrum of the generator.

It was just him and the soft green beret in his hands.

His father's beret.

"Bobo! . . . Bobo!"

Bobo looked up.

The Black Mamba was calling him.

The police chief leaned forward, searching Bobo as if trying to place him. Would the police chief recognize him from before?

"Go on, Bobo," said the Black Mamba. "Put on the ranger's clothes."

Bobo pulled on the jacket. He was not big enough for it and felt lost inside it. The sleeves came down over the tips of his fingers.

"And now the beret," said the Black Mamba.

Bobo gripped the beret to stop his hands from shaking. He pulled it on his head and stood tall.

The Black Mamba laughed and slapped Bobo on the back. "How do you feel, ranger?"

Bobo stiffened his back and nodded. "I will wear it with pride."

The White Lioness stood up and looked around the men. "Well, it is good to know my gorilla is in safe hands." She glanced at her watch. "That's all for today," she announced, bringing the meeting to a close.

The Black Mamba and the police chief followed her outside into the bright light. The police chief paused beside Bobo as he passed. He frowned. "Do I know you?"

"No, sir," said Bobo quickly. Too quickly. The police chief leaned closer and narrowed his eyes.

Bobo continued staring straight ahead, avoiding the police chief's gaze.

The police chief was searching his face, trying to place him. A fly buzzed close to Bobo's head, as if inspecting him too. Any moment now, the police chief would remember their meeting back at home.

"One more thing Mr. Mutombo," interrupted the White Lioness. "When I return next week, I need papers to show that the gorilla is fit and has a license for travel. I wouldn't want to be stopped by the authorities. Could you arrange that for me?" She tapped the briefcase in the police chief's hand. "There is more where this came from."

The police chief turned away from Bobo and nodded. "It can be done."

"Good," said the White Lioness. "I will be back next week for the gorilla."

Bobo took his chance to step back into the shadows of the hut and watched them walk away. The White Lioness and Clarkson climbed into the helicopter; the pilot started the rotor blades turning, lifting the helicopter up into the sky. The police chief glanced back once at Bobo, before he and his bodyguards disappeared into the darkness of the forest.

The camp resumed the steady rhythm of miners digging coltan, the *tink tink tink* of metal on stone, and the constant humming of the generator, as if nothing had changed.

But for Bobo, his world had turned itself inside out.

He held the beret against his chest and knew

without any doubt that his father was never coming back.

He knew deep in his heart that Papa was dead.

Bobo walked into the forest, slashing at the vines as he went. He walked deeper and deeper until he could no longer hear the sounds of the camp, until he was quite alone. He sank down, took the beret in his hands and buried his face in the cloth, in the smell of his father, and let the tears fall. He wanted to curl up, and become smaller and smaller and disappear.

"Bobo?"

Bobo sat up and spun around. Imara was watching him, Kitwana wrapped around her chest.

She sat down near him, placing Kitwana on the ground where he pulled at some leaves and nibbled them, glancing between Bobo and Imara.

"So, your father was a ranger?" said Imara.

Bobo nodded. "My father was a brave man. This is his beret."

Kitwana shuffled close to Bobo and sniffed at the beret in his hands.

"And this is your battle," said Imara. "This is why you came here?"

Bobo nodded. "The police chief lied. He said my father joined the rebels. He told a lie to stop ranger patrols near the mine."

"So what are you going to do?" asked Imara.

"I am going to prove my father's innocence."

Imara picked up a stick and scratched Kitwana's back. "The police chief is a powerful man. Why would anyone believe a kadoga, a child soldier like you? They will kill you first."

"I will get proof," said Bobo.

"How?"

Bobo put the beret back on his head. "My father's camera is somewhere in camp. It wasn't with his belongings when the Black Mamba emptied out his bag, but it will be somewhere. Someone must have it. I need to take a photo of the police chief with the Black Mamba. I need to prove he is corrupt."

Imara watched Kitwana climb along the length of a sapling. The trunk bowed with his weight until he scrambled up into another tree, staring intently into the forest. Imara followed his gaze but couldn't see what had caught his eye.

"Why do you tell me all this?" she said. "I could go to the Black Mamba right now and tell him who you are."

Bobo shook his head. "I know you won't."

Imara shrugged her shoulders. "You are nothing to me."

Bobo let a small smile escape. "Maybe not, but Kitwana is everything to you." He looked right into Imara's eyes. "Help me, and I can give Kitwana back his freedom."

Imara turned away from him. "You don't know me."

"I know you are a good person, Imara," said Bobo. "My father once told me that to know a person is to see how they look after their animals. I see how you care for Kitwana. I see the person you are inside."

Imara stood up, reached for Kitwana and scowled. "I have the devil inside me."

Bobo scrambled to his feet and stood in front of her. "Wait," he said. "I need to find that camera. It is the only way to prove my father's innocence. Can you help me?"

Imara stopped, her hand resting on the branch. She picked at some moss. "I don't know where it is," she said. "But if anyone has it, Rat has it. He was the one to bring your father's belongings back. I think I saw him carry something off into the forest. But even if he has it, I don't know where he keeps it."

"I know where it is."

Bobo and Imara spun around. Saka crept out of the shadows. Bobo aimed his gun, looking around them. "Who else is with you?"

"No one," said Saka, stepping out into the light. "I'm alone."

Bobo walked a circle around Saka. "How did you follow us?"

"I can track anything in the forest, even you," said Saka.

Bobo lowered his gun. "Do you really know where Rat keeps the camera?"

He nodded and cleared his throat. "If I tell you, you must promise to take me with you when you escape from here."

"Escape?" said Imara, looking between them. "Where will we go?"

Bobo frowned. "When I have the proof, we'll leave here for good. We'll take Kitwana with us, too."

"What will happen to him?" said Imara.

"The rangers will look after him at the orphan center for gorillas," said Bobo, "but if they can, maybe they will set him free."

"Free?" Imara held Kitwana close and ran her fingers through his fur. "If the Black Mamba catches us, he'll kill us."

Bobo nodded. "I know. But we have no choice." He looked at Saka. "The police chief will return next week when the White Lioness comes back to collect Kitwana. I need to take a photo of the police chief with the Black Mamba at the coltan mine. If you find me the camera, you can escape with us."

"And Frog," added Saka. "He comes too."

Bobo frowned. "No one must find out about this."

"Frog won't tell," said Saka. "We are like brothers."

Bobo stared at Saka for a moment, then nodded and stood up. "Where is it? Where does Rat keep the camera?"

Saka fiddled with the vine snare looped over his shoulder. "It's in a tree not far from here," he said, "a hollow tree, where Rat hides all his possessions. I have seen the camera in there too."

imara

You stupid girl, Imara. What are you thinking by helping him?

Imara walked ahead of Bobo back to camp, trying to ignore the demon screaming in her ear. Saka had already slunk back into the forest and disappeared.

You owe them nothing.

Kitwana struggled in her grasp as she returned to camp, reluctant to leave the playground of the forest. Imara held him closer, stiffening when she saw Rat standing in the shadows, watching her return.

Rat knows! Rat knows! Stupid girl. Stupid girl.

Imara heated water for Kitwana's milk. She watched him playing in the woodpile, pulling out sticks and tearing the bark with his teeth. He was growing stronger every day. In the forest he liked to climb the trees and vines. Sometimes Imara would play a game of chase with him round and round the trees until he climbed up so high that she couldn't reach him. He liked to forage for his own food too, although he always loved his milk and the close comfort of being held.

"Come on," called Imara. She grunted like Bobo had taught her, and Kitwana held up his arms to be picked up. She carried him away from camp to a high ridge overlooking the mine. The Black Mamba had built a wooden platform so that he could watch the workers. The platform was empty today, so Imara walked out onto the ledge and sat down with her legs swinging over the edge. As Kitwana took his milk, Imara looked down into the mine. It was busier than ever. There were even more men,

241

digging farther into the red soil, picking at the scab of the earth, not allowing the wound to heal.

The mine had spread wider and deeper. Some trenches had been worked so far into the ground that miners disappeared down dark holes, with head flashlights to guide their way. From up on the platform they looked like ants; working, working, working. But then Imara saw Saka and Frog, standing close together. Frog was pretending not to notice Saka, but he had stopped digging, his shovel held in midair and his head bent low toward Saka, whose mouth moved quickly, forming urgent words. And as Frog listened, his eyes grew wider and wider and wider.

You see . . . he is telling Frog about escaping. They are not careful. They cannot hide their friendship. Rat will see and destroy them. He will destroy you, too.

Imara lay in her hut that night listening to the laughs and shouts of men drunk on banana beer. Kitwana was asleep beside her, warm against her body, his fingers curled into her hand. She became aware of footsteps around the hut, padding softly toward the door.

Imara held her breath.

A sliver of moonlight cut through, as the door opened and a figure slipped into the room.

Imara reached for her panga. "Who's there?"

"Shh! It's me, Frog."

Imara could just make out his shape silhouetted against the night sky. "What are you doing here?"

Frog crawled into the hut.

Imara sat up and pressed herself against the back of the hut. "Get out."

"I want to thank you," he whispered, "for giving us the chance to go home."

"Who says you are going home?" snapped Imara.

"Saka said we are escaping with you and Bobo. We are going home."

"Shh!" hissed Imara. "Keep your voice down. No one must know. Do you understand?" She glanced through the open door. The men were sitting around the fire, drinking. She thought of the dawn raid on Frog's village. "What makes you think there's a home to go back to?"

Frog moved closer. "I saw my auntie hiding in the grasses with my brothers. The soldiers didn't see them. Maybe Mama was with her too. Maybe they are waiting for me."

See, sneered the demon, **even Frog has people who love him.**

Frog folded his arms around his knees. "Imara . . . ," he said.

Imara held her breath at the sound of her name.

"I wanted to say that you could come home with us."

Imara felt the devil inside her become still, listening.

"With you?" she said.

Frog nodded. "Mama takes in orphans from the wars. She took in Saka after rebels killed his parents. She cares for all children. She would care for you, too."

No one could love you, Imara. You stood by and watched Frog's family die. You have me inside. No one could love you.

"Get out," said Imara.

"I have this for you," said Frog. He leaned forward, pressed something into her hand.

Imara looked down at a tiny white flower in her palm. It seemed to glow bright in the moonlight; its fragile petals were pointed like a star. She looked up but Frog had already slipped out into the night.

Could she really find a home with Frog and Saka?

The demon paced circles deep inside. Circles . . . circles . . . circles. **You have nothing.**

You are nothing.

No one could want you.

Imara crushed the flower into the dirt.

She held Kitwana close, feeling his little body curled in sleep, safe against her. Kitwana still had a family. He belonged here in the forests. Bobo said he could give Kitwana his freedom.

Maybe she could somehow find freedom, too.

The demon gnawed inside her. **You can't escape, Imara. There is nothing for you outside this camp. There is no one for you. If you let Bobo take Kitwana, you will lose him forever, and then you will have nothing left at all.**

CHAPTER TWENTY-SIX

bobo

The next day, Bobo slipped out into the forest to meet Saka. He sank down onto the ground, hidden from view behind the buttress roots of a tree and waited.

Saka appeared with a small bundle in his arms.

"Have you been followed?" asked Bobo.

Saka shook his head. "We are safe here," he said, handing the package to Bobo. "I have checked."

Bobo took the bundle and unwrapped the camera. He turned it over and over in his hands. "Are you sure Rat won't know it's gone?"

Saka picked at a forest vine and twirled it in his fingers. "I don't think so. He never looks, he just adds more things to the tree."

"What things?"

"Bracelets, hunting knives, a pair of glasses, someone's shoe. He collects pieces of people's lives, things he takes from people on a raid, like trophies of war." He cast his eyes down. "I have seen a bracelet belonging to Frog's mama." Saka twisted the piece of vine so hard it snapped. "But I have not told this to him yet."

Bobo looked at the camera, Rat's trophy of his father. It held pieces of his father's life. With one flick of the switch he could see those moments. Saka crouched down next to him and watched.

Bobo turned on the camera. The display showed low battery. He would have to save the power, but Bobo couldn't resist a look. He played through the recent images Papa had taken of the Tumaini group. He saw Hodari, the silverback, resting in the leaves, being groomed by Hisani. Sunlight filtered through

the leaves and captured Hodari's expression, as if he was deep in thought. One photo showed Heri in her day nest, lying back with her face in the sun, her belly big from the baby growing inside. Several photos were action shots of Kitwana and Enzi, the blackback, chasing each other through the trees and mock-charging each other. Another showed Kitwana trying to run off with Papa's notebook and another of Hodari with his hand outstretched catching raindrops on his palm.

Bobo flicked through the images, trying to find the one he was looking for. Then he found it.

"Is that your father?" said Saka.

Bobo nodded. He stared into the photo he had taken of his father at home, his father with his beret at an angle on his head and his big wide smile.

Bobo stared into his father's eyes, so real on the image on the display. It seemed impossible to think that he no longer walked the earth or breathed the air. Impossible to believe he was gone. Bobo switched off the camera and held it to his chest, as if it held Papa inside, somehow keeping him alive.

"How are you going to take photos of the police chief without being seen?" said Saka. "The Black Mamba will expect you to be guarding him that day."

"I know," said Bobo, frowning. He turned the camera over and over in his hands. "But no one will notice if you aren't there." He paused. "Saka . . . ," he said. "Have you ever used a camera?"

Bobo showed Saka how to use the camera. Saka's eyes lit up at all the buttons and dials. Bobo showed him how to turn the zoom to make the image bigger on the screen. He showed him the battery pack and the memory card inside. "This piece of plastic stores all the photos," said Bobo.

Saka's eyes opened wide. "All of them?"

Bobo nodded.

"It's magic." Saka grinned. "You can keep a whole forest inside here. You can keep the *world* in here."

And proof of my father's innocence, thought Bobo.

He let Saka take some trial pictures and watched his face light up at the photos he had taken.

"That's enough," said Bobo. "We must save the battery."

Saka reluctantly switched off the camera.

"Make sure you get a photo of the police chief and the Black Mamba together," said Bobo. "Remember, make sure that you aren't seen."

"And I can still come with you when you escape? Frog too?"

Bobo nodded. "Can you get us across to the east of the mountains?"

Saka put his hand on his chest. "I am a Batwa. I know the forests. The forests are my home."

"Good," said Bobo. "Because once we leave, there is no going back. They mustn't find us. If they do, they will shoot us dead."

Bobo walked back to camp, collecting wild celery and nettles on the way for Kitwana. The image of his father stayed with him in his mind. Bobo could

252

almost imagine him walking next to him, his long easy stride, and his air of calm silence. Bobo felt it now. He felt his father beside him.

Rat was waiting for him outside the Black Mamba's hut. "Where have you been? The Black Mamba is looking for you."

Bobo dropped the leaves on the ground. "I was collecting food for Kitwana," he said. "He needs to eat."

Rat narrowed his eyes. "Where's Saka? He went into the forest too."

Bobo looked around. "How do I know where he is? I am not his keeper."

Rat followed him into the hut, keeping close behind. "I see you talking with the Spirit Girl," he said. "You are getting too close to her."

Bobo ignored him and joined the other Mambas standing in a circle around the Black Mamba.

"I'm watching you," Rat said to Bobo, loud enough for the Black Mamba to hear. "I'm watching you."

"You're late," snapped the Black Mamba.

Bobo stood to attention. "Sorry, sir." He could see Rat smirking in the shadows.

The Black Mamba nodded. "The Spirit Child doesn't need your help with the gorilla. Don't go near her again."

"No, sir," said Bobo. He swallowed hard, feeling the Black Mamba's glare linger on him.

"We have a problem," said Black Mamba, looking around the Mambas gathered in his hut. "Rat has discovered some of the miners hiding coltan and taking it out of the forest."

Rat puffed out his chest, his shoulders back, looking ahead intently.

The Black Mamba leaned forward. "I cannot have miners stealing my coltan," he said. "How has this been happening?"

The Mambas kept their heads down, not looking at him.

The Black Mamba banged his fist down. "You have been letting this happen under your noses. You are lazy, all of you," he yelled, "and drunk on beer.

You are not worthy to call yourselves Mambas." He swiped cups and pots from the table with his hand and looked around them all. "Don't let anyone steal my coltan again. Understood? You know what to do if you find them."

Rat smiled, a grin showing his row of broken teeth.

"We need more patrols in the mines," said the Black Mamba. "We need more checkpoints on the forest paths. Search everyone. Show no mercy. Coltan is valuable. Life is cheap." He paced in front of his men. "Where is the Spirit Child?"

"Playing with her monkey," said Rat.

"Bring her here."

Rat nodded and slunk out of the hut.

The Black Mamba wiped at sweat beading on his forehead. "There are people who want to kill me. I feel it," he said. "But you have all become lazy and drunk." He spun around looking at each one. "I have looked after you and this is how you repay me!"

The men were silent, staring at their feet.

The Black Mamba paced round and round, pointing at each of them with his finger. "Who feeds you? Who gives you guns? Who gives you power? You all need me. Without me you have nothing. Nothing! And yet you choose to sit and drink beer in the middle of the day. You are not worthy of being my men."

Bobo stared hard at the floor. He could hear a fly batting at the steel mesh on the door.

The Black Mamba kicked an empty beer can out of the hut. "There will be no more beer. If I see any of you doing nothing, you will be working in the mines. Is that clear?"

The Black Mamba's head jerked around as Imara slipped in through the door. He glared at her, his nostrils flaring with each breath. "Where have you been?"

"Feeding Kitwana," said Imara, keeping her eyes on the floor.

"Last night I saw an owl," he said. He paced around Imara. "An owl. It is a bad sign. A bad omen." He pressed his face close to Imara. "Why did you not warn me?"

Bobo could see Imara's fingers dig into Kitwana's fur.

"What is happening, Imara? The men are lazy, there is sickness in the camp, we have thieves among us, and there are some who want to kill me. You protect this gorilla, but you do not protect me."

Imara avoided the Black Mamba's eyes, but her hands were shaking. She couldn't hide her fear.

The Black Mamba took a step away from her. "Rat says you are losing your powers."

Bobo glanced across at Rat to see his lips curled upward in a sneer.

"Rat is wrong," said Imara. She stood up straight and looked at the Black Mamba, but her voice trembled with a harsh whisper. "I am your Spirit Child."

The Black Mamba touched his snake-bone amulet. "I hope so, Imara. Soon your gorilla will be gone. I wonder, will the spirits protect you then?"

CHAPTER TWENTY-SEVEN

imara

R at followed Imara, never letting her out of his sight. He became her shadow. He listened to everything she said. He stood beside her when she served out food to the Mambas so that she couldn't even talk to Bobo.

The mine was busier than ever before. The Black Mamba had docked three weeks' wages from each miner as a punishment for stolen coltan, and it seemed the miners worked harder, digging deeper and faster into the red earth. Soon the White Lioness would come to take away the coltan and she

would come for Kitwana too. Imara w
the mine's edge, aware Rat was tailing h
slung around his shoulder, a cigarette hang
the corner of his mouth. She watched the sac of
coltan being weighed and bagged, ready for the helicopter. Frog worked with new energy, digging into
the ground, his face alight with the promise of
home. She watched him shovel earth into the collecting pans, for washing and separating the coltan
from the mud. Imara could sense Saka and Frog's
shared excitement of the secret that sustained them,
connecting them like an invisible rope.

It was only when Imara walked through the forest to search for food for Kitwana that she managed
to give Rat the slip. She crouched behind a buttress
of tree root and watched Rat glancing this way and
that as he passed. Kitwana stayed close, gripping her
clothes, sensing the danger. Imara made her way to
the river where she knew the wild celery grew, and
sat down in a patch of sunlight, letting Kitwana play
in the trees. She watched him climb and hang upside

down. She could feel her mouth break into a smile as he chased a butterfly across the ground, spinning in circles as it spiraled out of reach. She lay back and breathed in the moment of quiet, the sunlight filtering through the leaves. Maybe she and Kitwana could slip away together into the forest. Maybe she could find his family. Maybe they would accept her as one of their own.

"Psst, Imara!"

Imara turned. She could not see anyone but recognized Saka's voice. He had come so close without being heard. Not even the demon inside her stirred.

Saka slipped from behind a tree and sank down beside her. "Rat is not far away," he whispered.

"What is it?" said Imara.

"Bobo said to ask if you are coming with us when we leave tomorrow."

Imara picked at the river grasses. She shrugged her shoulders. "Where would I go?"

"Frog says you can come with us."

Imara shook her head.

Saka put his hand on hers. "Come with us, Imara. This war is not your fault. You are lost, like us. You can escape with us too."

Imara snatched her hand away. "I can't escape, ever," she hissed, feeling the demon stirring deep inside. "Wherever I go, I can't escape the devil. I am his child."

"But you can't stay in the camp either," said Saka.

"I know," said Imara. She flicked the grasses into the river and watched them being swept away. "I have decided to go far away from here. I will go with the White Lioness if she'll still take me."

Saka looked across at Kitwana. "What about Kitwana? Will you take him too?"

Imara closed her eyes, squeezing back hot tears. She whispered softly so the demon inside would not hear her words. "Saka, I want Bobo to take Kitwana for me. Bobo said the rangers would look after him, maybe even release him with his family. If I have one wish, it is for Kitwana to be free."

Saka frowned and nodded. "We'll take him with us, if you won't come yourself. But there won't be much time. We must get him away from here soon after Bobo has proof of his father's innocence. If we don't, the White Lioness will take him with her when she leaves."

Imara nodded.

"Meet us here," said Bobo, pointing to the rock. "Meet us here with Kitwana, after Bobo has the photographs he needs."

Saka and Imara sat in silence watching Kitwana play. His attention focused on something deeper in the forest, his head bobbing side to side to get a better view. He stood up and patted his fists against his chest, giving short sharp warning barks. Imara scrambled to her feet to see Rat coming through the trees.

"He's here," whispered Imara. But when she turned, Saka had already slipped into the shadows and was gone.

"Who were you talking to?" demanded Rat.

Imara reached up into the branches and pulled

Kitwana into her arms. "To the devil, to ask him what he should do with you."

Rat stared back. "I'm not afraid of you," he said. "Your powers are weakening."

"What do you want, Rat?"

"The Black Mamba wants to see you," he said. "He is coming down with the sickness. He needs you to cure him."

Imara turned away from him and marched back through the forest.

Rat trotted to keep up. "You have to give your baby up tomorrow," he sniped. "Kitwana goes tomorrow. You won't have him anymore. What will happen to your powers then?"

Imara walked ahead of Rat and smiled. She wouldn't let the White Lioness take Kitwana. She felt as if she had more power than she had ever had before. She felt it surge, like a warming ray of sunshine, from her chest, down her arms and through her fingers, spinning a shield around Kitwana, keeping him safe. She would never let anyone hurt him. Bobo would take him and give Kitwana his freedom.

She turned and faced Rat, looking him right in the eyes. "Do not test my power," she said softly. "Not even I know what it can do."

The Black Mamba was lying on his bed with a blanket wrapped around him. His forehead shone with sweat and he clutched his snake-bone amulet in his hand. Bundi had left a concoction of pills on the table, but the Black Mamba had not taken any.

"Imara," he grunted. "I am dying. I can't trust anyone anymore. Help me. You must make me strong."

Imara sat down beside him. He had the sickness that swept through the mine, but he didn't look like he was dying.

He is not very sick, Imara, but let him think it is so. Show that you alone can save him.

"I will make you special tea," said Imara, placing a hand on his forehead. "You must drink plenty and you must rest." She made up the medicine from the powder into a large glass of water and held it to his lips to sip. "You will be strong again," she whispered. "I call on the spirits to protect you."

The Black Mamba lay back on his pillow. "You are good to me, Imara. But there are also bad spirits around here. Keep them away from me. Don't let them near me while I sleep."

He still needs you, whispered the demon. **If you tell him of Bobo's plans to escape he will reward you. You will be his Spirit Child forever. You will have all the power.**

Imara watched Kitwana playing with an empty beer bottle trying to stick his tongue inside and taste the sweet liquid.

"I can't," she whispered to the demon. *"I do this for Kitwana, not for you."*

Imara watched the Black Mamba drift into fevered sleep, then lifted Kitwana in one arm and left to make his bottle of milk. The day was hot and muggy, pressing in. Imara wiped her face with a cloth and slapped at the insects that buzzed and tried to settle on her skin. She poured boiled water into the milk powder and shook the bottle. Kitwana climbed into her lap, reaching up to take the bottle in his hands. He put it to his lips, and Imara smiled as she watched him guzzle the milk, his nose twitching as he drank.

Rat sat in the shadows watching her. "Your baby is even uglier than you," he sneered.

"Haven't you got work to do?" said Imara, without looking at Rat. "The Black Mamba said anyone sitting around would be sent down to the mines."

"He asked me to keep a watch on you."

"The Black Mamba trusts me," she said.

"For now," said Rat. "But I will find a way to test your loyalty."

Imara ignored Rat and put the empty bottle into a pan of water boiling over the fire, the way Bobo had shown her to clean it. She stared into the water. It seemed impossible to think that tomorrow Kitwana would be free. Bobo, Saka, and Frog would be free, too. She thought of them running into the forest, and wished that she could join them. Frog had said she could live with his family. Maybe she could. Maybe? Saka was not Frog's kin and yet his family had taken him in. Hope swelled up inside her. Tomorrow, she decided, she would escape with them. She would hold on to Kitwana and run with Bobo, Saka, and Frog. She'd run with them, far away from here, deep into the forest. Tomorrow she and Kitwana would be free.

She watched a bubble forming at the bottom of the pan. It was small at first, a tiny bead of vapor crushed by the weight of water, but it pushed outward getting bigger and bigger, rising up and up until it burst through the surface, escaping into the air.

"IMARA!"

Imara looked up. Saka stood in front of her, wide-eyed. He was puffing and panting, trying to catch his breath.

Rat was on his feet. "What is it?"

"There's been a landslip at the mine," Saka gasped, clutching his sides. "Two men are buried."

He turned to Imara. "Frog is buried too. The walls collapsed on him."

"Take me there," she said. She glanced at Kitwana playing happily with the logs and hoped he'd stay until she returned.

She and Rat ran, following Saka toward the mine. They scrambled and slithered into the gulley where Frog and the other men had been working. Imara couldn't see any sign of the other two men, but Frog was trapped, clamped beneath the landslide. Only his head and shoulders and one arm were free above the mud. Bobo was working with other miners to dig Frog out, but as fast as they cleared the soil, more slid down from the steep bank.

Frog was gasping for breath, rasping air deep into his lungs.

Rat jumped down beside him and pushed Frog's chin up with his foot. "Pah! He is dead already." He turned to Imara. "Let him see your face so he may die more quickly."

Imara knelt down beside Frog.

Saka crouched down next to her and held on to Frog's free hand. "Don't leave me," he whispered. "We are going home, remember? You and me. We're going home."

Frog was struggling to breathe. Spittle frothed in the corner of his mouth.

"Stay with me," pleaded Saka. He gripped Frog's hand tighter. "We're going home. We'll walk the cattle to the river again. We'll cool our feet in the water like we used to do. We're going home."

Imara tried to clear the soil that trickled down across Frog's face. His lips had turned smoke gray.

"Imara, do something," whispered Saka.

Imara looked at the weight of mud that held Frog trapped. Half the hillside had slipped down upon him.

Rat kicked a pile of earth. "Frog will die," he said, walking away.

Imara leaned forward. "Frog," she whispered, "can you hear me?"

"Emmanuel," said Saka to Imara, his voice

shaking. He said the name more clearly. "His name is Emmanuel."

Imara bent down to Frog, her face inches from his. "Emmanuel?"

Frog looked up at her with wild, scared eyes. "Mama?"

Imara looked into his, but he was staring beyond her to somewhere she couldn't see.

"Mama?" he said again.

Imara put her palm against his face and spoke so quietly, that only Saka and Emmanuel could hear.

"Emmanuel," she whispered, "your mama is coming for you." She stroked his forehead. "Do you see her, Emmanuel?"

Emmanuel nodded, and managed a smile through his rasping breaths.

"See, she is waiting for you," said Imara. "Now go. Go home to her. Run into her open arms."

Imara and Saka held Emmanuel as his last breath left his body.

Imara briefly touched Saka's hand, then walked

270

away, while Rat stood back to let her pass, a smile on his lips. "You care for them." He laughed.

Imara ignored him.

"I have found your weakness, Spirit Child," he called out. "I have found your weakness. You have no protection now."

CHAPTER TWENTY-EIGHT

imara

*I*mara sat in her hut and fed Kitwana a bottle of milk. She tried to block out thoughts of Emmanuel, but she kept seeing him in her hut, offering her the small white flower. He had offered her his friendship. He had offered her a home.

Emmanuel is dead, the demon reminded her.

Imara closed her eyes and tried to force out the memory. Only yesterday she had dreamed of leaving the Mambas to live with Emmanuel and his family, but now those hopes had died with him.

Kitwana was fidgety, and kept pushing the bottle

away. Imara knew he sensed her restlessness. He was desperate to get into the forest and play and forage for food. But this morning was different. This morning the White Lioness was coming to camp. Kitwana clambered about the hut pulling the blanket from Imara's sleeping mat and screaming indignantly when she tried to grab it back. He tore at the strips of wood on the door.

Imara opened the door and let Kitwana outside. It had rained steadily all night and the sky looked thick with clouds. Maybe the White Lioness wouldn't come today. She'd heard Bundi say the helicopter pilots avoided flying through the storms.

The camp was busy. Rat was ordering men around, piling up the full sacks of coltan ready for the helicopter. Water ran and dripped from the trees and carved out new gullies in the scoured valley, sending thick brown water churning downstream. Imara looked around for Saka. He had disappeared into the forest soon after Emmanuel's body had been buried and no one had seen him since. Maybe he had already escaped, now that he no longer had his friend to look after.

Bobo was pacing circles near the sacks of coltan. He seemed preoccupied, stopping and then moving position. Imara cast her eyes around the camp. Bundi was inspecting the coltan, weighing the sacks and making notes on his clipboard. The steady *tink tink tink* of tools and the scraping of the earth of miners at work rose up from the mines. Imara watched Bobo. He paced another circle and glanced up into the branches of the nearest trees. She followed his gaze. High in the canopy layer, she saw Saka stretched out across a branch. For one moment she had seen his leg swinging, but now it was still and Saka was almost invisible again, almost part of the tree. He was holding the camera in his hands, pointing it in line with Bobo. So this was where Bobo had planned to set up the photo of the police chief and the Black Mamba. Imara looked back at the camp. She didn't want to give Saka's position away.

She wondered how she would get Kitwana to

the meeting point. She had to get him away from here. If Kitwana left with the White Lioness, Imara would never find him again. Maybe Imara could leave now, walk through the forests in search of food and be ready and waiting to meet Bobo and Saka.

Imara pulled on her cape and took Kitwana's hand, letting him lead her toward the forest path.

"Imara!"

Imara turned. The Black Mamba was calling her, looking recovered from his bout of sickness.

"You look better," said Imara.

The Black Mamba nodded. "See, the spirits have protected me. I am well again."

Imara turned to follow Kitwana into the forest.

"You must stay here," called the Black Mamba. "The White Lioness is on her way. She will want her gorilla baby soon."

"I am only taking him for a last feed," said Imara.

The Black Mamba shook his head. "There is no

time. Come with me," he ordered, "and be here to welcome her."

Imara lifted Kitwana in her arms and stared longingly into the trees. She'd missed her chance. If she'd left moments earlier, she'd be away in the forest by now. She followed the Black Mamba to Bundi and the piles of coltan at the trading shack next to the flattened ground where the helicopter would land. She walked past Bobo, as if he wasn't there. Bobo ignored her too, but she could feel his tension and she felt bound to him and Saka; three points of a triangle, connected by their thoughts. Rat slunk into the middle of the triangle, looking between Imara and Bobo, but neither would give him the satisfaction that they acknowledged each other. Kitwana tried to reach out for Bobo, but Imara pulled him away and walked on.

The radio in the Black Mamba's hand crackled to life, and Imara could hear the pilot's voice telling him they would soon arrive.

Imara felt Kitwana's grip tighten. He had sensed

the helicopter before her. The clouds above pulsated with sound and then the helicopter emerged from the whiteness, in a roar and whirl of rotor blades. For a moment it swung wildly in a strong gust of wind, before the pilot brought it down to rest.

The White Lioness climbed down from the helicopter and picked her way across the mud, careful to keep her pale khaki trousers clean. She waited for Clarkson to join her and hold an umbrella for her to walk beneath.

Imara felt sick as she watched the Mambas unload a large, sturdy crate with ventilation holes cut into the sides. So this was Kitwana's cage. This was how Kitwana would leave the forest. The Mambas carried it up to the trading shack and placed it next to the coltan waiting to be stacked.

The White Lioness walked straight to Imara, her arms outstretched for Kitwana. "Let me hold him." She smiled.

Imara gripped her hand tightly around Kitwana. The White Lioness pulled something from her pocket. "Let's see if he wants to try a toffee."

Kitwana took the toffee from her and poked his tongue out, tasting the sweetness. Then he put it in his mouth and rolled it around inside, poking his finger in his mouth, trying to dislodge it from his teeth.

"Come," said the White Lioness, "let me have him."

Imara reluctantly let the White Lioness take Kitwana from her and feed him another toffee. It became a game to Kitwana and he pushed his fingers in her pockets to look for more.

The White Lioness flicked back her hair. "I knew I'd win him over in the end. He is just like all men." She laughed. "You have to find out what they want first."

The demon inside Imara twisted and turned.

"And you," the White Lioness said to Imara, "have you made your mind up? Are you coming with me?"

Rat was standing next to them, listening.

"If the Black Mamba is willing, I will," said Imara.

The White Lioness smiled. "Black Mamba," she called, without taking her eyes from Imara. "How much for your Spirit Child? I want to take her, too."

The Black Mamba walked a circle around Imara. "What do you want with her?"

"She is interesting." The White Lioness raised an eyebrow. "I like interesting things. Besides, I need her to look after the gorilla."

"She is our Spirit Child. She protects the men."

A smile curled at the corners of the White Lioness's mouth. "I would have thought a man like you would be strong enough to protect your own men."

The Black Mamba said nothing, but Imara could see a small blood vessel pulsing on the side of his forehead.

"I'm sure you will find another Spirit Child," said the White Lioness. "I can make it worth your while."

The Black Mamba glanced at Imara and rolled the snake-bone amulet beneath his finger. "No," he said. "She is not for sale."

The White Lioness shrugged her shoulders. "Well, maybe I will be able to persuade you before I leave." She looked around the camp. "Where is the police chief? Where are the papers he promised me? I need documentation to take the gorilla with me."

The Black Mamba scanned the forest edge. "He should be here soon."

The White Lioness tutted. She looked up at the sky and held her hand out to feel the rain falling as a misted drizzle. "I don't like to be kept waiting. The pilot says the weather is closing in and we must leave before the afternoon."

The Black Mamba nodded. "Come," he said. "Come and keep dry until he arrives."

Imara followed the White Lioness, Rat, and the Black Mamba along the path to the Black Mamba's hut. She was aware of Bobo walking close behind her. He shoved her, elbowing her out of the way, and as he passed he bent his head and whispered hastily, "I need them all out in the open when the police chief gets here. Try to get them all out by the gorilla cage so Saka can take the photo."

Rat whipped around. He narrowed his eyes at Bobo and Imara, but Bobo ignored him, walking straight ahead.

Imara made coffee and brought it to the Black Mamba's hut. She watched the White Lioness playing hide-and-seek with the toffees. Kitwana was too wrapped up in the game to notice Imara. Somehow she had to get him away before the White Lioness loaded him up in the crate.

The rain drummed harder and harder on the hut roof and water found its way through tiny holes. The steady drip, drip, drip of water on the floor marked the passing of time. The White Lioness glanced at her watch. "Clarkson," she said. "Make sure the coltan is loaded and check with the pilot when we must leave."

Clarkson pulled his hood up and stepped out into the rain. The White Lioness tutted. "I will have to go soon whether your police chief is here or not."

Rat appeared at the door. "The police chief is arriving."

"Good," snapped the White Lioness, standing up. Imara tried to reach for Kitwana, but he had already climbed into the White Lioness's arms looking for more toffee.

"I can carry him," said Imara. She tried to lift Kitwana from the White Lioness, but Kitwana shrieked at her. He wasn't going to let Imara take him away from his hoard of toffees.

The White Lioness smiled, looking at Kitwana. "It's all right. I'll hold him." She stroked his cheek. "See? He knows I'm his mama now."

Imara trotted close behind the White Lioness, with the demon screaming in her ear all the way. The last few sacks of coltan were being loaded up. The crate for Kitwana was open and ready for him. Imara glanced at Bobo. She knew he needed a photo of the police chief and the Black Mamba out here, so she stepped in front of the White Lioness. "Come," she said. "Let me help you put him in the crate."

Clarkson walked over from the helicopter. "The pilot says we must leave. There are electrical storms forecast. We must get out now."

"Wait, I need the forms for the gorilla," said the White Lioness.

The police chief staggered up the hill toward them, his feet slipping and sliding in the mud. Imara could see that he tried to maintain some dignity by wiping his face, but he only smeared more mud across it.

The Black Mamba and Bundi joined them. The Black Mamba and the police chief were in position. Imara wondered if Saka had a clear view. For a moment, the rain eased and wide puddles shone in a shaft of sunlight. Yet the clouds were swollen with more rain, and thunder rumbled across the mountain.

"You are late again," the White Lioness said to the police chief.

"It was the rain. The roads were bad—"

The White Lioness cut across him. "I am not interested in excuses. I want the forms."

The police chief reached into a bag slung around his waist and pulled out some papers protected in a clear plastic envelope.

The White Lioness took them from him and scanned the writing. "Good," she said. She clicked her fingers for Clarkson to fetch a small briefcase from the helicopter. "Give him the money, and then let's go."

Imara couldn't take her eyes from the crate. She wanted to grab Kitwana and run, but it was impossible. The White Lioness had hold of Kitwana and she wasn't going to let him go.

Clarkson handed the briefcase to the police chief and turned to leave.

"Wait," said the police chief. "I need to check it's all here." He opened the case. The Black

Mamba peered in to see it packed with dollar bills.
Thunder rolled around the mountain.
A bright white light lit the sky.
But it wasn't lightning.
It was the automatic flash of a camera.

CHAPTER TWENTY-NINE

imara

The Black Mamba looked up and squinted into the tree. Rat was already running and pointing his gun into the canopy.

"It's the Batwa boy!" he cried. "He has a camera!"

Imara watched to see Saka fumbling with the camera, trying to keep hold of the branch.

"Come down before we shoot you down!" roared the Black Mamba.

"Who is taking photos?" shouted the police chief. "You have spies among you!"

"Come down!" shouted the Black Mamba,

firing a warning shot into the tree.

Imara watched as Saka scrambled down. She felt sick deep inside. **I warned you!** screamed the demon. **I warned you what would happen!**

The Black Mamba pushed Saka to the ground. "What are you doing?"

The police chief grabbed the camera and thrust it in Saka's face. "Where did you get this? Who are you spying for?" He dropped the camera, swung his rifle butt and smashed it, bringing it down, blow after blow. Still not done, he picked up the pieces and threw them into the fire where they crackled and sparked in the heat. Imara watched the plastic melt and buckle. Bobo's evidence was gone. She glanced at Bobo, but he was staring hard at the ground.

"Get up," roared the Black Mamba. He leveled his gun. "I knew I had a spy. Who set you up to this?"

"No one," mumbled Saka.

"Liar!" shouted the Black Mamba, spit flying from his lips. He pushed his face close to Saka's. "Who are you working with?"

Rat sidled next to the Black Mamba. "Don't forget it was Imara who said the boy should live. Maybe they are in this together."

The Black Mamba spun around.

Imara took a step back.

You fool! Rat knows your weakness. I can't protect you now.

"What do you know of this?" said the Black Mamba.

"Nothing," said Imara. "It is the powers of the spirits that let him be caught."

"She lies," sneered Rat. "She cares for him."

"He is nothing to me," snapped Imara.

The Black Mamba narrowed his eyes and Imara bit her lip, sensing she had protested too much.

Rat leaned closer to the Black Mamba. "Maybe if she chose to give him life, then she can be the one to end it."

The Black Mamba took a deep breath and nodded. He handed Imara his rifle. "Do it."

Imara stared at the gun.

"DO IT," shouted the Black Mamba.

You see! screamed the demon in her ear. **You are losing everything . . . Emmanuel, Kitwana, Saka, and Bobo, too. You have nothing. You are nothing. This is all your fault.**

"IMARA!" The Black Mamba pushed the rifle in her hand. "Kill the boy."

Imara lifted the rifle to her shoulder. The demon inside her squirmed and clawed. **Do it, just do it. It makes no difference who pulls the trigger. Saka is dead already.**

Imara looked into Saka's face. His eyes were wide, wide open, staring straight ahead. His teeth were clenched together and his cheeks puffed in and out with shallow quick breaths.

Rat was sneering beside her. "Do it."

Imara lifted the gun higher. It felt heavy in her hands. She couldn't stop trembling. She closed her eyes and swallowed hard. When she opened them, she was looking down the barrel of the rifle at Saka, pointing it right in the middle of his chest.

imara

Do it. Do it now.

Imara breathed slowly in and out, trying to slow time with each breath. She tried to allow her thoughts to settle and block out the demon screaming in her mind. She felt her blood pumping through the palms of her hands. A trickle of sweat traced a downward path along the length of the scar, dripping onto her neck from her chin. The world began to blur and distort. The air became thick and silent. Everything seemed slowed and slurred, as if trapped in time. The woman with the coffee-colored skin walked through her thoughts, between Saka and the end of the gun. Imara blinked. The woman turned and smiled before slipping into the forest and disappearing in the dark spaces between the trees.

Imara lowered the rifle. "It is not right to do it here. His spirit will infect this land and bring bad luck."

"She lies," said Rat.

Imara turned to the Black Mamba. "It must be done outside the camp, far away from here."

The Black Mamba stared at her.

Be careful. You have lost his trust.

"It is the only way," said Imara. "His ghost will not leave you unless you do."

The Black Mamba nodded. "Then do it." He took back his rifle and turned to Rat. "Take Imara and the boy into the forest and do it there."

Imara looked around. The White Lioness was closing the lid on Kitwana in the crate. His arms stretched through the slats of the crate reaching out for her. Imara wanted to run and pull Kitwana away, but there was nothing she could do.

Rat gave Imara a shove. "Move," he ordered.

She turned for one last view of Kitwana before Rat marched her and Saka deep into the forest.

As soon as they were out of sight of the camp, Rat pushed Imara ahead with Saka. "I don't trust you, Spirit Child. I may as well kill you both. I'll tell the Black Mamba that you tried to escape. I'll say you are a spy, too."

Rat kept them moving through the forest path until they reached the clearing by the river.

"Here will do. Now sit, both of you," he barked. He aimed his gun. "Hands on your heads."

Imara sat down on the damp ground next to Saka, knocking her elbows against his as they raised their hands.

"Good." Rat smiled. He lowered his gun and leaned against a tree. "Now what I want to know . . . ," he said, pulling a cigarette from his pocket and lighting it with one hand, ". . . is who put you up to this?"

Imara and Saka remained silent.

"I'll find out one way or another," said Rat, breathing smoke into the air. "Who put you up to this?"

"I did!"

Rat spun around.

Bobo stepped out into the light and aimed his rifle at Rat's chest before Rat had a chance to lift his own.

"Don't," warned Bobo.

"You haven't got the guts to shoot me," taunted Rat. "You're a coward. A boy pretending to be a man."

"Saka, take his gun away," ordered Bobo.

Rat reached for the gun, but Bobo fired a shot. It sank into the tree with a dull thunk of splintered wood.

Saka lifted the rifle from Rat and joined Bobo, leaving Rat curled in fear on the ground.

Bobo walked in a slow circle around him. "You are the coward. Now you have no gun to hide behind." He looked across at Imara. "What about you, Imara? Are you going to come?"

Imara thought about Kitwana. Had the White Lioness left already? Maybe she could get back in time. "My loyalties lie back at the camp," she said.

Bobo nodded.

He turned to Saka. "Let's go."

Imara watched as Bobo and Saka slipped into the forest and were gone. She wanted to run with them, away from Rat and the camp, but the thought of Kitwana held her.

"You knew," said Rat.

"No," said Imara. "Why didn't I go with them?"

"The Black Mamba will not protect you now," he said.

Imara glared at him. "And I will tell him how you let them get away. Maybe he will think you are a spy, too. He will not be pleased with you."

Imara marched ahead of Rat, desperate to find Kitwana. She hadn't heard the helicopter yet. Maybe the White Lioness hadn't left. She imagined Kitwana locked inside the crate, curled in a ball, trying to block out the world. Above, the sky had darkened and a sudden squall of wind whipped the branches, scattering the leaves and twigs. Thunder rumbled in the far distance, a forewarning of the coming storm. Imara broke into a run, her feet sliding on the mud, a living nightmare of three steps forward, and two steps back. Maybe she would be in time, but as she emerged from the trees, the downdraft from the helicopter rotor blades pushed her back, as it lifted up into the sky.

Imara could see the White Lioness's pale face staring down at her.

"Kitwana!" she screamed. She ran through the mud, reaching upward, clawing the air, but the helicopter disappeared into the clouds, taking Kitwana from Imara and the forest, to the Land of Money, far, far away.

CHAPTER THIRTY-ONE

imara

The Black Mamba smashed his fist against a tree. "Bobo and the Batwa boy escaped?" he spat. "There are spies everywhere. We must send men out to hunt them down."

Imara thought of Saka. If Bobo stayed with him, they would both be safe. Saka knew the forests; he could slip into the spaces no one else could see. The Mambas wouldn't be able to find them.

The police chief paced in circles. "I know the tall boy," he said. "I remember him now. He is a ranger's son. His father was the one you killed." He stopped and pressed his finger on the Black Mamba's chest. "He knows me. That boy must not get back to the town. At any cost."

"Rat," ordered the Black Mamba, "take men into the forest and don't come back until Bobo and the Batwa boy have been found and shot."

The police chief glanced at his watch. "I need to get back," he said.

One of his bodyguards leaned closer. "It is too late to travel, sir. Too risky with the money."

The police chief nodded. "We will leave at first light tomorrow." He turned to the Black Mamba. "We'll stay in camp tonight."

Imara watched the police chief take a seat and settle in the Black Mamba's cabin. The Black Mamba raged about the camp, kicking pots and pans looking for a quarrel.

"Bundi," he bellowed, "why are there no men in the mines?"

"There is too much water in the mine," said Bundi.

The Black Mamba turned on him. "Did I say there is too much water? Get the men back in there."

The Black Mamba stormed up to his viewing platform, watching men scrambling down the slopes into the mine.

Imara slipped away and crept into her hut, half expecting to see Kitwana curled up on her blanket chewing on strips of bark. But her hut was empty. Only the crumpled red dress remained, a reminder of the White Lioness's promises. Imara picked it up and tore the silk, ripping it with her hands. She didn't stop until the dress was in shreds of fabric on the floor.

Imara curled up into a tight ball, bringing her knees up to her chest. She wrapped her arms around herself. She longed to feel Kitwana's hand grip hers and feel his small body curled up against her. She felt his loss like a deep pain, as if part of her had been torn apart.

The demon settled inside her. **I told you not to**

**let them in, but you did, didn't you! You didn't lis-
ten. And now they've all left you. Why would
they stay for you? You have nothing, Imara. You
are nothing. No one could love you.**

Thunder rumbled over the mountains, the deep
echoes bouncing across the valleys. The storm was
getting closer. Imara could feel it through the
ground. She willed it to get louder and louder, to
drown out the demon and the sound of the scream
building up inside her. She wanted the thunder to
tear apart the mountain. She wanted it to swallow
up the mine, the Black Mamba and everything in it,
even her. She wanted to bury it all deep beneath the
earth.

Above the sound of thunder, someone was
hammering at Imara's door. She pulled the blanket
from her head to see Rat enter the room.

He kicked her sleeping mat. "Didn't you hear the
Black Mamba? The White Lioness is coming back."

Imara sat up. "Coming back? Why?"

"There's bad weather over the mountains, and
it's coming this way. The mzungus will have to stay

the night. The Black Mamba said you are to make up some beds in his hut and get food ready for them."

Imara pulled on her boots and glanced at Rat. "You are back so soon from the forest. Did you find Bobo and Saka?"

Rat kicked the door, but avoided Imara's eyes. "Of course," he spat. "I killed them both."

He lies, whispered the demon.

Imara smiled inwardly. *I know.*

She stood up. "That's good news," she said. "The Black Mamba wouldn't want to hear of their escape."

Rat stood in the doorway, grinding his teeth together.

Imara pushed past him. "Close the door after you. Don't let the rain in my hut."

Above, the sky was coltan gray; the dark clouds sagged closer to the earth. Imara collected charcoal and built up a fire. There was no bush-meat now that Saka had left, so Imara set up a pot boiling with rice and beans.

All the time, Imara kept her eyes and ears to the sky, waiting for the helicopter. She heard it before she saw it, the low thudding shaking the air, the rotor blades fanning the flames of the fire. She watched it come in to land, swinging in the swirling winds. It landed with a hard bump, the landing skids sliding in the mud.

Imara left the fire and moved closer. The pilot opened the door for the White Lioness and Clarkson. The White Lioness carefully picked her way across the mud.

"We will have to stay overnight and leave at dawn," she said to the Black Mamba. She fiddled with an earring and glanced between the helicopter and the makeshift camp.

She is scared, whispered the demon. **She is stuck here and that frightens her.**

"Where is Kitwana?" said Imara. "I'll give him his feed."

The White Lioness brushed her away. "He'll be fine in the crate until tomorrow."

"He will need his feed," insisted Imara. "He will get sick otherwise."

The White Lioness wiped at the rain on her face and pushed back her hair. Her eye-paint ran in thick black streaks down her cheeks. "Very well," she snapped. She pulled her coat tighter around her. "It seems I'm going to be stuck here for the night, so where am I expected to sleep?"

"This way," said the Black Mamba.

The wind chased the White Lioness and the Black Mamba into his hut. Imara hurried back to the helicopter. She could see the wooden crate inside, beside the sacks of coltan. The pilot was busy in the cockpit, so Imara hauled herself up into the belly of the helicopter. She scrambled over sacks of coltan to the crate and untied the thick nylon straps holding down the lid. She reached into the crate as Kitwana reached up for her. He pulled himself close to her, curling his fingers around her neck, giving small hoots and groans of relief, trying to press himself into her as if he could become part of her. Imara buried her face into his fur and breathed in the smell of him. He belonged here, to the forest, not to the Land of Money. Whatever happened, she would never let him go again.

She wrapped him in a blanket and carried him close to her, tying the ends of the blanket around her chest. She walked with him across the cleared ground, the wide puddles, sticky and red with mud. The clouds had sunk lower, pressing down on the camp. It was late afternoon, but the sky was dark. It glowed with deep violet light. The air was charged with electricity and the promise of a storm. Despite the Black Mamba's orders, men were leaving the mines for the safety of their makeshift shelters and tented camps. She could see the miners securing their tarpaulins with heavy rocks. Even the Mambas had taken to their shelters. Imara was the only person to be standing outside in the open, with Kitwana clinging to her.

Above, bolts of lightning chased each other across the sky. Thunder rocked the ground beneath

Imara's feet. She looked across into the Black
Mamba's hut where the White Lioness was hiding
from the storm, watching her. Maybe the people in
the Land of Money could hide from storms like
this. But not here. No one could hide here. Its
power made equals of men.

Imara felt the storm rage within her too. Rain
began to fall, hard bullets of water hammering the
ground and pummeling her skin. The wind roared
through the canopy of leaves. It surged like a vast
river of air, the trees bending and groaning beneath
its weight.

Imara knew the whole camp was watching her.

She stood fast in the middle of the clearing, a
lone figure lit up by strobes of lightning.

Imara threw her head back and raised her arms
up to the sky.

She spread her fingertips out wide and willed the
storm to show its power.

CHAPTER THIRTY-TWO

bobo

Saka didn't stop until he had led Bobo across two deep ravines to the east side of the mountain. Bobo had heard the shots from the soldiers following them, but the gunshots were always far away. He'd found it hard to keep up with Saka's steady jog, scrambling over tree roots and ducking beneath vines and branches.

But Saka knew the animal tracks and the river crossings from his hunting trips into the forests. He had kept up a fast pace even as the light faded and the storm raged above them. The storm had become their protection, allowing them to get away. When it became too dark to see anything at all, Saka pulled Bobo beneath an overhang of rock. The ground was damp, but it was sheltered from the wind and rain. Bobo pressed himself against the rock and wrapped his arms around his knees. Neither of them had spoken since their escape.

"I'm sorry," said Bobo. "I shouldn't have put your life at risk like that."

Saka switched on the small flashlight he kept in his pocket. He shone the yellow light in Bobo's face. "We are free," he said.

Bobo shook his head. "No one will believe me when I get home. It is my word against the police chief's. There is nothing to prove his guilt. The proof was burned with my camera in the fire."

"Don't be so sure," said Saka. He pushed his fingers in his mouth and pulled something from the inside of his cheek. He shone his flashlight on a small square of blue plastic, the metal strips catching the light. "Is this what you wanted?" he said.

Bobo leaned forward, eyes wide. He took it from him, turning it over and over in his fingers as if trying to make sure it was real. "The memory card from the camera!" He looked up. "But how?"

"I knew they would take the camera from me," said Saka. "So, I slipped the memory card out before I climbed down the tree." He paused. "Only I didn't think I would ever get away."

"Did you get the photo of the police chief and the Black Mamba?"

Saka nodded. "I'm not sure, but I think so."

Bobo wiped the dampness from the memory card and slipped it into the inside pocket of his jacket. He shook his head slowly from side to side. "This could change everything, Saka. Everything."

"It was worth risking my life for," said Saka.

Bobo felt the corners of his mouth break into a wide smile, stretching muscles he hadn't used for some time. "We are going home," he said. "And I am going to prove my father was an innocent man."

* * *

It was late the next evening when Bobo and Saka found the main logging road that cut between the mountains. They managed to climb unseen aboard a logging lorry heading east, scrambling up to hide between its cargo of huge tree trunks, while the driver was picking his way slowly through a pot-holed section of the road.

Saka slept while Bobo lay awake watching the forests recede into the distance, the mountains silhouetted against a storm-drained sky. The lorry picked up speed along the straight roads toward the city, only stopping once at a trading hut for the driver to show his papers. Away to the east, the lights of the town glowed dull orange. Saka woke and stared wide-eyed at the beginnings of the town, criss-crossed with electricity wires. They passed buildings with steel-shuttered windows and long straight roads busy with traffic. The headlights of cars and trucks glared in their eyes as they passed.

When the lorry stopped at a junction, Bobo gave Saka a shove. "Come on, jump down; I think I know my way from here." Bobo led them through the maze of streets, keeping in the shadows. He paused at the entrance to his school, dark and locked up for the night. It seemed a lifetime ago that he'd left, and impossible to wonder if he could return as a student there one day.

Saka rubbed his bare feet. "How do you find your way in the city?"

Bobo laughed. "How do you find your way in the forest?"

"Are you going home?" asked Saka.

Bobo shook his head. "My mother and brother and sister had to leave. We are going to see the only person I know I can trust."

"Who?"

"Kambale, my father's boss," said Bobo. "He will know what to do."

Lamu peered out from behind his father, his eyes wide. "Bobo! What are you doing here?"

"Can we come in?" said Bobo.

"Of course," said Kambale, ushering Bobo and Saka inside. He glanced up and down the road before shutting the door.

"Who's this?" said Lamu, taking a step away from Saka.

Bobo tried to answer, but he felt his head spin. His knees buckled and he crumpled to the floor.

Kambale called to his wife. "Marie! Bring some blankets and some food too for Bobo and his friend." He crouched next to Bobo. "Rest first, Bobo; then tell us your story."

Bobo shook his head. "No," he said. "There is not much time. I need to tell this story now."

Kambale's wife fussed around them, sitting them down on floor cushions and wrapping blankets around Bobo's and Saka's shoulders. She fetched them each a bowl of hot stew.

Kambale pulled up a chair. "What is it? What have you come to tell me?"

Bobo reached into his jacket for the green beret. He held it out with shaking hands.

Kambale took it and turned it over and over, tracing his fingers around the bullet hole. He looked up at Bobo. "I am so sorry."

Marie folded her arms around him.

"My father was innocent," said Bobo. "I have been in the rebel camp. I have proof."

Kambale leaned back. "The other side of the mountain is out of bounds. The Black Mamba rebels are too dangerous. The police chief says it isn't safe to go there."

"I have just seen the police chief there," said Bobo. "He is in the pay of the Black Mamba." Bobo put his hand into his pocket and slipped out the memory card. "I have proof to bring the police chief down."

Kambale glanced at his wife.

Marie shook her head. "It wouldn't surprise me. I hear he has bought another house on the other side of town, and another in Kinshasa, but ay . . . ay . . . ay . . . he is a powerful man. I wouldn't want to cross him."

Kambale stood up and walked to the windows. He pulled the curtains closed. "I have my work laptop here," he said. "Let's see what is on the memory card."

Bobo and Saka sat next to Kambale while his laptop came to life, the blue screen lighting up the room. Saka stared, transfixed.

Bobo gave the card to Kambale. "I hope it's not damaged."

"We'll soon find out," said Kambale. He pushed the card into the slot and waited. Bobo fiddled with the corner of the blanket. Maybe the photo wouldn't be in focus. Maybe it wouldn't show the police chief. Maybe it wouldn't come out at all.

The images came up on the screen, and Kambale scrolled through until he reached the one he was looking for. The photo was clear and sharp. Kambale sucked air sharply through his teeth. There was no doubt about the man standing with the Black Mamba, staring into a briefcase full of dollars. It was Mr. Mutombo, the chief of police.

Kambale leaned forward to get a closer look at a young gorilla held by someone half hidden behind the police chief. "Is that Hisani's son?"

Bobo nodded.

Kambale peered more closely at the photo. "But who is holding him?"

"A foreigner," said Bobo. "You can't see her face."

"Hisani's son is alive," whispered Kambale.

"A girl in camp looks after him. She calls him Kitwana." Bobo shook his head. "But I think he has been smuggled out of Congo already."

Marie looked over Bobo's shoulder. "Ay, ay, ay, Bobo! The rebel camp! You are lucky to be alive."

Bobo smiled at the small Batwa boy. "It was Saka who saved me. I'd never have escaped without him."

Kambale breathed out slowly. "What do we do? Who do we tell that the police chief is corrupt?"

Marie glanced at the windows and the doors. "Keep your voice down," she whispered. "The police chief and his guards are powerful men."

Kambale drummed his fingers on the table. "We need to make sure this photo reaches enough people. We can't let this image disappear. But it is difficult to know who to trust."

Lamu spoke up. "What about the army?"

Kambale stood up and paced the room. "There are many in the army just as corrupt."

Marie sat back in her chair and folded her arms. "Then you must trust his biggest enemy. Find the man who wants to bring the police chief down."

"General Mulumba," said Kambale. "It's plain knowledge that there is no love lost between the general and the police chief." Kambale sat back at the computer and opened up his emails, his fingers poised to type. "I'll send this photo to the United Nations and the conservation groups I know, and then I'll try to see the general."

"There is no time to lose," said Bobo. "The police chief may still be at the camp. Mulumba will find him there."

Kambale nodded. "I'm sure the general will want his victory."

Bobo got to his feet. "I must go back."

Kambale looked up. "Go back?"

"For the girl, Imara," said Bobo. "I must go back."

Kambale put his hand on Bobo's shoulder. "I will tell the general about the girl and the gorilla. I will ask him to keep them safe, but I can't let you return."

"I have to," said Bobo. "They need me."

"I will take you to your mother," said Kambale. "Your family needs you now. You can't go back into the forest. There is no more you can do."

Bobo shook his head. "No," he said. "I didn't do enough to save them."

"Bobo," said Marie, putting her arms around him, "you have done more than enough. You have proved your father's innocence."

CHAPTER THIRTY-THREE

imara

The storm had raged into the night, battering Imara's hut, tearing through the trees. Imara had curled up with Kitwana, feeling his body against hers. He clung even harder, his fingers gripping onto her clothes, while she had slept a restless sleep. She had thought of escape, of running into the forest to try to follow Bobo and Saka, but it would have been impossible to get away. The Black Mamba had ordered Rat to guard her hut.

"Get up," said Rat, pushing open her door. "The Black Mamba wants to see you."

317

Morning light cut through onto the floor. Imara pulled her blanket around her shoulders and lifted Kitwana into her arms. She blinked in the bright light. Outside, the sky was clear and blue, the air cool and fresh. Small clouds fringed with golden sunlight hung in the pale dawn sky. In the west, a few stars still clung to the night.

Imara looked around at the aftermath of the storm. Trees on the edges of the cleared forests had come down in the night, their huge roots upended and exposed. The river in the deep gorge churned red with mud washed from the crumbling banks and the lower trenches of the mine had flooded. But Imara couldn't take her eyes from the flattened part of the ground where the helicopter should be. The helicopter had been blown over in the storm, and had slid into a deep trench, its rotor blades digging into the thick mud. The pilot and Clarkson were thigh-deep in mud, inspecting the damage.

The Black Mamba grabbed Imara's arm. "You did this," he hissed.

Imara shook her head. She tried to pull away, but the Black Mamba dug his fingers deeper.

"You conjured the storm," he said, his eyes wild. "We saw you. We all saw you."

He doesn't trust you anymore.

"Am I losing you, Imara?"

Imara gripped Kitwana against her. "No. I am your Spirit Child."

The Black Mamba pulled her close. "I will kill you before I let you go."

The White Lioness marched across to the Black Mamba, ignoring Imara and Kitwana. She held her phone in the Black Mamba's face. "I need to charge my phone."

The Black Mamba shook his head. "The generator isn't working."

"I'll use the radio instead."

"There's no signal," said the Black Mamba. "Storm damage."

The White Lioness pushed her hair from her face and glared at the Black Mamba. "I need to get out of here," she said. She lit a cigarette. Her hair had lost its gloss and had turned the color and texture of dried grass. She looked older to Imara too, her eye-paint smudged, her lips pale, her skin deeply lined.

She breathed out pale blue smoke, the hand holding the cigarette shaking slightly and the other hand turning the cigarette packet over and over and over. "Can you fix it?" she called to the pilot.

The pilot looked up. "I think so. We need to tie some ropes to pull it back up again. But I don't think we can leave today. Tomorrow maybe."

"Another night?" the White Lioness snapped. "Another night in hell." She turned and marched back to the Black Mamba's cabin.

The Black Mamba loosened his grip on Imara. "Go and make some food for me. Watch Imara," he called to Rat. "Don't let her out of your sight."

Imara slipped past with the bag of maize for porridge. She turned her back on Rat and built the fire, scattering some of the maize beside her for Kitwana. As she stirred the porridge, she watched Kitwana sitting on the ground, his legs tucked under him, picking up maize between his finger and thumb, carefully inspecting each flake before putting it in his mouth. She glanced into the soft darkness of the forest. Maybe she could slip away, but Rat was watching her, his leg jiggling up and down as if waiting for her move.

Imara carried a pot of coffee and a pan of thickened porridge to the Black Mamba's hut and served it into cups and bowls. The men ate their porridge quickly, scraping around their bowls with their spoons. The White Lioness stirred hers, but didn't touch it, leaving it to go cold. "Isn't there any decent food in the forest?" she demanded.

The police chief put his empty bowl on the ground and glanced at his watch. "We must go soon," he said, his hand resting on the briefcase full of money. "It will take half the day to walk to the jeeps."

The White Lioness shook her head. "No, you have to stay. You will escort me if the helicopter doesn't start. I need your protection."

Imara watched a frown line form on the police chief's forehead. He sipped his coffee, watching her.

On the other side of the river, Imara could see the miners and their families begin the day. Smoke rose up from their fires; women shook out blankets and tent covers to dry from the night before. The miners climbed down into the sections of the mine that hadn't flooded and fell into the rhythm of another day.

But the camp had changed.

Imara could feel the tension. The White Lioness stayed in the Black Mamba's hut, insisting on an armed guard outside her door. The police chief lit one cigarette after another, pacing outside the hut, while the Black Mamba walked up to his viewing platform to oversee the mine. Imara could see him standing with his hands behind his back, silently watching the miners. He stared straight ahead, unmoving, but as she watched she could see he twisted the snake-bone amulet round and round and round, counting the bones beneath his breath.

The day stretched out long and slow. Imara was glad of the evening when she could return to her hut with Kitwana and curl up beside him. The helicopter had been pulled from the mud and the pilot had said it was fit to fly, but it had been too late in the day. The pilot planned to leave the next day at first light.

Imara pulled the blanket around Kitwana, drawing him closer. His chest rose and fell in steady sleep. But Imara couldn't sleep. The roar of last night's storm was replaced by silence. Deep silence, as if the forest was waiting and holding its breath. As if the forest held a secret, and knew that everything was about to change.

imara

Gunfire shattered the dawn, spiraling birds into the sky.

Kitwana woke, clinging to Imara. She could feel his heart thumping in his chest. His eyes were wide with fear.

Imara tried to calm him, grunting to him and stroking his fur, but his fingers gripped her, pulling himself closer.

Rat burst into her hut. "Get up, get up."

Imara sat up. "What is it?"

"Government troops! The army is here."

Imara scrambled to her feet. Through the door she could see Mambas pulling on jackets and boots and ammunition. More gunfire crackled from the trees beyond the mine. Miners and their families were spilling out from their tents and running away into the darkness between the trees.

The White Lioness emerged from the hut and looked wildly around. "Clarkson!" she yelled. "We must go."

The Mambas spread out along the camp and lay on the ground, their guns pointing toward the forest edge. A shell from a rocket launcher shrieked over Imara's head and exploded deeper in the forest, splintering the trees. The shockwave threw her to the ground, forcing Kitwana from her grip. The camp had turned to chaos. Mambas flitted between the trees taking up new positions to attack. The police chief stood back in the shadows searching left and right for his escape, the briefcase of money clutched against his chest.

The Black Mamba was on the platform over the

mine where he fired down at the troops in the forest. Imara saw him standing at the top, the orange flare of his rifle pumping shots. For a moment, he looked invincible, one man against an army. But he had no protection from the bullets. He was just a man. She heard another round of gunfire from the forest and watched the Black Mamba as he crumpled and fell forward, spinning over and over, cartwheeling into the flooded mine. Imara stared as the waters closed over him. Ripples spread outward and a few bubbles rose and broke the surface. Then all was still. The Black Mamba had finally gone.

Imara turned around to see if Rat had seen him fall, but Rat had already fled. She saw his feet flying up behind him as he ran away from camp, deep into the cover of the forest.

Maybe this could be her escape, too. She pulled herself to her feet and held her arms out for Kitwana, but someone else lifted Kitwana up instead. The White Lioness whisked him away before Imara had a chance to grab him.

"Give him back!" yelled Imara.

The White Lioness was already running, her head bowed low, toward the helicopter. The rotor blades were spinning, Clarkson and the pilot already inside. Kitwana's arms were reaching out for Imara. He shrieked above the sound of gunfire.

Clarkson reached down to pull the White Lioness and Kitwana up into the helicopter.

Imara ran and launched herself forward, wrapping her hands around the White Lioness's knees and they spun and slithered across the mud. Imara grabbed Kitwana and pulled him close.

The White Lioness pushed herself up, reaching out for Kitwana. "Give him to me."

Imara glared back. "He's not yours to have."

The White Lioness grabbed Kitwana's arm and tried to pull him from Imara, but Kitwana sank his teeth into her hand.

She pulled back, holding her bleeding hand with the other. "Then come with me too," she snapped.

Imara backed away, Kitwana clinging to her. "No."

Gunfire cut through the air around them, bullets smattering like rain into the puddles. Behind the White Lioness, the helicopter was lifting up into the air, its skids hovering just above the ground, ready to leave.

The White Lioness flinched at the sound of bullets hitting the metal sides of the helicopter. "It's your choice!" she yelled above the roar of the engine and rotor blades. "If you come with me, you and Kitwana will live. If you stay, you die."

Imara glanced at the dark spaces between the trees, her mind racing along the pathways deeper and deeper into the forest.

"I have another choice!" she shouted, holding Kitwana close against her, and tensing all her muscles to run. "And I choose freedom."

gorilla

Kitwana clung to the Girl Ape, feeling the sky-colored eyes of the Pale Ape staring at him. His heart thumped in his chest as the fire-sticks crackled around them, flashing back to memories of the silverback falling. The Pale Ape had tried to take him, but the Girl Ape had held on, and Kitwana listened to their strange yabberings and shrieks as they faced each other, eyes locked. Kitwana had sensed the danger, sensed the Pale Ape wanted to take him like she had before, and he had fought back, sinking his teeth into the Pale Ape's hand.

The Girl Ape backed away and Kitwana buried his face

329

in her chest and clung tight as she ran. The trees splintered and the ground broke up, exploding around them, but still the Girl Ape ran. It was not until the sounds of the fire-sticks faded that she fell to her knees and curled up, wrapping herself around Kitwana.

It was long after the sun had passed its highest when Tall Apes found them. These were Tall Apes that Kitwana hadn't seen. New Killer Apes. They had chased the other Tall Apes away and sauntered through the camp, their shoulders back, their heads up high. The sharp, sweet smell of blood and fire-sticks hung in the air.

These new Tall Apes led the Girl Ape away and she followed willingly, along paths out of the forest. Kitwana clung to her, not wanting to let go, wanting to hold the only one he could trust. But at the forest edge, the Tall Apes yabbered soft noises and Kitwana felt the Girl Ape's arms release him as she let them take him from her. Kitwana fought to cling to her, but the Girl Ape turned her back and walked away. He tried to dig his teeth into the Tall Apes holding him, but the Tall Apes held him and all Kitwana could do was watch the Girl Ape leaving him, like his mother had before. He was alone again. Fear rose up inside him He shrieked for the Girl Ape, but she didn't seem to hear him. She just kept on walking and didn't look back. She kept on walking out of the forest, away, away.

CHAPTER THIRTY-FIVE

imara

Open your eyes, Imara.

Imara held her eyes shut tight.

Open your eyes. See, after all, that you have nothing. You are nothing. You lost Kitwana. You knew you would.

Imara pulled the blanket over her head, trying to block out the demon, but the demon would not be quiet.

Open your eyes.

"Open your eyes, Imara. There is nothing to fear."

Imara felt the blanket being lifted from her. She

opened her eyes and looked at the woman sitting beside her on the bed.

The woman leaned forward and smiled at her. "My name is Comfort."

Imara clung to the blanket and stared.

Comfort was a big woman, with a smile to match. "Welcome to Halfway House," she said. "You are safe here. This is your home, for now."

Imara looked around. She had arrived late the night before and fallen into sleep in the soft darkness. Now morning light flooded the room she found herself in. It was a large room. The paint-flaked walls were clean and bright. Some twenty beds were crammed side by side, each one occupied by a girl or young woman.

Imara could feel them watching her, and closed her eyes again.

Comfort put her hand on Imara's shoulder. "Do you want to talk, Imara?"

Imara buried her head in her pillow.

"Give it time," said Comfort, standing up. "You can find me when you are ready."

Imara pulled the blanket over her head and tried to force herself to sleep, to escape the images of the battle. She relived it, over and over in her head, when the troops had finally taken over the Mambas. The troops had found her and told her that Kitwana would be taken to a gorilla orphanage where he would be looked after. She had known that she couldn't keep him. She had known it was best for Kitwana, but it hadn't made it easier walking away from him. Leaving him. His screams still echoed in her mind, mixing with the cries of babies in the room.

Imara peered out from beneath the blanket and looked along the row of beds. Many of the women here had babies. Some mothers didn't look much older than her. She watched them hold their babies close and feed them, the babies' small hands grasping and clinging and looking for comfort. Imara hugged her pillow against her chest. She tried to imagine Kitwana, the shape of him, his smell, and the way he wriggled to get free to run off and cause mischief. But Kitwana was gone, and she would never see him again.

You have nothing. It's just us now, you and me. Don't let anyone close again. Remember, you are mine, Imara. You are the devil's child.

Imara tried to stay in bed and avoid the other women, but Comfort wouldn't let her. After the other women had washed and dressed and left the room, Comfort came back to find her.

"You cannot stay in bed forever, Imara," said Comfort, handing her a small trowel. "The vegetable garden needs to be weeded. Everyone must do a job here, if we all want to be fed."

Imara sat up and swung her legs out of the bed. She put her hand up to her face to hide the scar.

Comfort put her hand on Imara's. "You are not the only one to have a scar. Many girls here carry theirs inside. There are many who will have experienced the same things you have."

She doesn't know anything about you.

Imara tried to turn away, but Comfort held her for a moment. "Here we help girls learn to read, to write, to grow vegetables, and to sew," said Comfort. "Here they learn to mend themselves. They learn to live. Life can begin again here. It can begin for you, too."

She lies. There is nothing left for you, Imara. Nothing.

Imara left Comfort sitting on the bed and walked outside, feeling the hard pebbly ground beneath the soles of her feet. She felt a hundred years old, bone-bent and weary. She made her way to the small patch of ground where she could see some of the women working their way along rows of beans, onions, and potatoes. In the distance, low hills broke up the flat line of the horizon. She looked back at the concrete building of Halfway House. It sat on the edge of a town. The corrugated iron roof was riddled with rust and holes, and the walls were cracked and pockmarked. A washing line of bright clothes lifted gently in the breeze. It seemed so far from the rebel camp. Here she could see people smiling and laughing, sharing stories and jokes. Yet, Imara couldn't join them. She felt cut off, different from the rest. What they shared seemed inaccessible to her. She found it hard to feel anything at all.

A woman in a bright yellow dress beckoned her over and pointed to the row of newly planted beans. Imara crouched down on the earth beside them. The shoots were pushing above the earth, the small leaves bright and new. They looked so small, so fragile they could be crushed before they had a chance to grow. Imara copied the woman and pressed sticks into the ground to encourage the thin tendrils to curl around and take hold. It felt good to be doing something, working the earth with her bare hands. It was as if her hands already knew what to do, as if they had done this work before. While she worked, she became lost in the moment. Even the demon became settled and drowsy inside her.

Comfort brought out a drink and sat beside her. "You like working in the garden?"

Imara nodded.

"Maybe tomorrow you would like to help the other women with the cooking? Or join the sewing group?"

Imara shook her head. "I like it outside," she said. She glanced at Comfort and could tell Comfort knew she wanted to be on her own.

"When you're ready," said Comfort, standing up and brushing soil from her skirt, "come and join us. You will find friends here."

CHAPTER THIRTY-SIX

imara

In the following days, Imara worked in the garden and watched the small bean shoots curl up around the sticks. They seemed to grow so fast that she could almost see them reaching for the light before her eyes. Every day, they grew thicker and stronger. Imara weeded and watered them, determined to keep them all alive. The hot sun warmed her back and neck. The red soil crumbled beneath her fingers. As the day warmed up, she lay down beneath the row of tomato plants and looked up through the leaves. They spread out above her like

the canopy of a miniature forest. She closed her eyes and breathed in the heavy scent of green growth, imagining Kitwana clambering up the trees and chasing butterflies through shafts of sunlight.

"Imara?"

The demon stirred, pulling Imara from her daydream.

She opened her eyes and looked up to see Comfort hurrying between the rows of tomato plants. Sweat glistened on her cheeks and pooled in damp patches on her dress beneath her armpits. She stood over Imara, puffing and panting.

Imara sat up. "What is it?"

"There are some people here to see you," said Comfort, mopping sweat from her brow.

"Who?"

"Come, child," said Comfort, helping Imara to her feet. "They want to ask you questions. They have some news for you."

Imara followed Comfort back into the rest house, trotting to keep up with her. The other women and girls stopped their work to peer out from doorways at her. Imara kept her head down to avoid their stares.

"Come into my office," said Comfort, "it's quieter there. They are waiting to meet you."

Imara stopped in the doorway. Two people, a man and a woman Imara hadn't seen before, were sitting in the room. The woman was a mzungu like the White Lioness, only this woman was younger, with soft brown hair. They both turned to Imara and smiled.

"Come in," said Comfort, "come into my office."

Imara stepped in and looked around the room. She hadn't imagined Comfort to have a room with a desk, a computer, and a phone. She had only seen Comfort cooking and cleaning and looking after the girls in her care. Books and files lined the back of the room and on one wall, a photo of each girl was pinned to a board. On the far side of the room, a door led from the office to another room. The door was slightly ajar and Imara could hear the scrape of a chair across the floor and low murmurs from the other side.

Comfort glanced at the door and pulled it shut. "Please sit, Imara."

Imara sat and stared down at her hands, where the mud had caked in a hard crust on her skin.

Comfort pulled her chair closer to Imara. "These people are Zoe and Mbera. They are from a charity that helps children like you, children of war."

Imara glanced at Zoe. On the cover of a file on her lap lay a photo of Imara. The demon recoiled inside her.

What are they doing here?

Zoe leaned forward. "How are you, Imara?"

Imara clenched her hands shut tight and fixed her eyes on the flakes of mud that collected in the creases of her skirt.

The mzungus can't be trusted.

Mbera cleared his throat. "We understand that you were living in the camp of the Black Mamba and his men."

Imara felt her mouth go dry. It became hard to swallow.

"The Black Mamba is dead," said Zoe.

Imara nodded. She had seen him die.

"It is important that you know his rebel group is finished," said Mbera. "We have come to tell you this."

This is not why they are here.

Zoe ran her fingers around the edges of the file. "The mining in the park has stopped too. The park is safe again. The police chief is in prison awaiting trial for corruption and smuggling coltan to Rwanda."

"And the White Lioness?" said Imara. "What about her?"

Zoe glanced at Mbera and shrugged her shoulders.

"The mzungus," said Imara. "What happened to them?"

Zoe flicked through her files and frowned. "I don't know. . . . We have no record. . . ."

Imara twisted the frayed hem of her skirt in her fingers. "So they got away?"

Comfort took Imara's hand in hers. "Who did?"

**Forget about the White Lioness. They are not
here because of her.**

Imara shook her head and pulled her hand away.

She wanted to ask about Bobo and Kitwana, but
the room felt hot and stuffy. A fan whirred on the
ceiling but barely moved the air. Footsteps paced up
and down on the other side of the door. A shadow
flitted across the gap between the bottom of the
door and the floor.

The demon paced inside her mind. **Get out of
here, Imara. There's something in that room you
mustn't see.**

Imara stood up. Her palms felt slick with sweat.
"I have work to do," she said. Out of the corner of
her eye she could see the handle of the door slowly
turning.

The demon hammered on her chest. **Get out
now!**

"Wait," said Zoe, standing up. "There is something else. Do you recognize this man?"

Zoe handed Imara a photo of a wiry man with hair braided like rats' tails.

Imara's hand trembled as she held the photo. "Rat," she whispered.

She traced her fingers down her scar. It felt raw and wide, wide open.

She could feel the demon shrink back inside.

So this is why they are here.

CHAPTER THIRTY-SEVEN

imara

Zoe tapped her fingers on her file, not taking her eyes from Imara. "This man is in prison too, but he's hoping for a lenient sentence by giving the army information."

Imara stared at the photo. So Rat was trying to buy his freedom. She crushed the photo in her hand. "He should never be let out."

Mbera took the crumpled photo from her. "He has told the police of the location of all the villages the Black Mamba plundered."

Imara looked up at him. "That would take a long time. A *very* long time."

"It did," said Mbera. "Many of the villages lost children to the war." He leaned forward and searched her eyes. "One of the villages lost a girl, a young girl who was on the way to market with her brother."

The demon filled Imara's head. **Don't listen to him.**

But Mbera continued, speaking softly. "The young girl's name was Imara."

Don't listen! Walk away.

Walk away!

"Shut up!" shouted Imara. "Shut . . . up."

"Imara," said Zoe.

Comfort put her hand on Imara's arm.

Imara backed away. "SHUT UP!" she screamed. "You don't know anything."

Run, Imara, run.

But Imara couldn't run. She couldn't breathe. The far door had swung wide, wide open. Walking through the doorway came a woman, hand in hand with a tall boy.

Imara felt the demon dig his claws into her heart.

Close your eyes, Imara. Close them now.

"Imara?" the woman was calling her name. She was the woman in her dreams, the one with the coffee-colored skin. But here she looked solid. Real. Of this world, not the spirit one.

Imara felt the demon crush her lungs. She closed her eyes and tried to suck in air. "No! You're in my head. You're in my dreams. You are not real."

"Open your eyes."

Imara dug her fingers into her palms. She felt the woman's hand on her shoulder. "Open your eyes, Imara."

Imara forced her eyes open. She looked at the woman and the boy, trying to place them.

She felt the demon twist her heart round and round, the pain exploding in her chest. Her knees buckled and she crumpled onto the floor.

The boy knelt down beside her. "Don't you recognize me?" he said softly.

Imara searched his face, seeing a younger boy behind his eyes.

"I was with you when Innocence died," he said. "I am your brother, Kitwana."

"Kitwana!" gasped Imara. The demon was swelling inside her chest, giving no room to breathe.

The woman pulled Imara up into her arms and buried her face in Imara's hair. "My child," she whispered.

Imara tried to push her away. "I have the devil in me. I am his child."

"No," whispered the woman. "You are *my* daughter. You are no one else's child but mine."

Imara gripped tightly to her mother. She could feel the demon swell and grow, pushing outward on her ribs, squeezing tears out from her eyes.

"Let it go," said Imara's mother. "Just let it go."

Imara felt her mother's arms around her and she did; the demon surged from her, down through her arms and through her fingertips. She felt hot tears falling down her face. She wrapped her arms around her mother and clung on tightly, wanting to hold her there forever.

"My child," whispered Imara's mother. "There is no demon inside you. There never has been." She wiped Imara's tears and held her face, looking deep, deep, deep into her eyes.

"What has been trapped inside of you all this time . . . is love."

PART TWO

now . . .

CHAPTER THIRTY-EIGHT

imara

My name is Imara Kizende.

I have returned to the village where I was once a child. The scattering of huts with their mud walls and banana-leaf roofs lies in a small valley a half-day's truck ride from the forests. Here, the green hills are terraced with fields of banana, potatoes, beans, and cassava. Cattle graze by the river, swishing their tails and flicking their ears at the flies, while the boys looking after them splash in the water. A few eucalyptus trees cling to the hillsides, their gray mottled branches reaching up to the sky.

Mama tells me this is where I belong.

She has spread a sleeping mat for me on the earth floor of her hut, next to Embe, the sister I had not met before. When I sleep, Mama lies beside me in the darkness and soothes the night terrors that wake me. She tells me I am safe here.

She tells me this place is home.

For the first few days I stay inside, curled in darkness, facing the walls with my eyes closed. I hardly eat or drink. I hear villagers call by. Babu, my father, talks to them and tries to persuade me to come outside, but I don't want them looking at me. The scar is my history written on my face. There are things I don't want anyone to see. I just want to be alone. The devil no longer speaks to me. He has left and in his place is silence. An unbearable silence. I want to lie my head in the dust and sleep. I just want to sleep forever.

But Mama won't let me sleep. One morning she opens the door and lets the early morning light in. She sits beside me, stroking my forehead.

"Come," she says. "Come and help me pick beans for market."

I feel her hand slip into mine and let her lead me out into the bright, bright sunshine. My legs feel weak beneath me. I follow her up through the fields, the broad cassava leaves brushing my legs. I walk close behind Mama, wanting to reach out and hide myself in the folds of her skirt, but I am much too big for that. Embe runs ahead, hiding behind the tall banana plants to peer out at me, at the sister she has never known. The villagers stop in their work and I feel their eyes on me as I pass. I keep my head down, watching my feet tread into Mama's footprints in the rich dark soil.

Mama stops in her field, beside a row of beans, her basket propped against her hip. She tilts her head to one side. "Do you remember this, Imara? Do you remember picking beans with me?"

I stare at the basket and shake my head. I don't remember anything. My mind feels empty. Stripped bare, like fire-scorched earth.

Mama puts her hand on my cheek. "Then we will start again," she says. She picks a long green bean and drops it in the basket. "We will start again."

I fall into her rhythm, reaching for the beans and filling the basket, as she works her way along the row. The sun warms my back and the air is filled with Mama's soft humming. It feels familiar. Safe. I have been here before. But it was so long ago it feels more like a dream.

We finish picking the beans and Mama sits down, patting the earth for me to sit next to her. I sit down and wrap my arms around my legs and look down to the village. There are women working in the cassava fields below us, their bright skirts like flowers against the dark green leaves. Babu is working away, building roads farther north, and Kitwana is in school in town. He proudly tells anyone willing to listen that he is the first person in our family to go to school.

Mama takes my hand in hers and holds it tight.

"I never imagined this day," she says. "We are blessed to have found you, Imara."

I try to smile, but I'm not sure I have yet been found. I shade my eyes against the sun and stare down the long dusty road that runs next to the village.

The road where my old life ended.

I try to remember the day Innocence died. I try to remember for how long I have been lost. All I know is that Kitwana was a small boy then, but now he is as tall as me.

I became lost the day my world was lost to me. I can only see it now through my brother's eyes, but as I retell his story inside my head, I am not sure if they are all his memories or if some of mine are finding their way through. I try to find my way back to that day. If I close my eyes, I can see the midday sun high, high in the sky. I can feel the trickles of sweat on my forehead running down the sides of my nose and in the creases of my mouth. The basket is heavy on my head as we walk home from market where I sold our cassava and tomatoes for a small bag of rice and three ripe mangos. The sweet smell of the mangos is heavy in the air. Kitwana is like a bothersome fly. He runs circles around me, trying to knock the basket from my head.

"Tsk!" I say. "These are for Mama. The baby will soon be here and Mama wants mangos. Babu said to make sure we bring some home from market."

Innocence, our neighbor, is far ahead. She has grumbled all the way. She says she has better things to do than walk with us to market. We are too slow, too noisy, too lazy. She says we laugh too much. Maybe she forgets Kitwana carried her bag of potatoes six miles to the town.

"Innocence has a thunderstorm in her head," says Kitwana.

I poke him in the back. "And a tongue like lightning. Don't get too close, or she'll strike you dead." I jab Kitwana in the arm. "Like that."

Kitwana laughs and runs ahead. "Look, Imara. It's true. See the clouds swirling around her. She is a thunderstorm."

I stop and steady the basket on my head.

Kitwana is right. Farther along the road a cloud of dust rises high into the air. It swirls in a column of red and yellow into the clear sky. It's moving fast toward us, like the dust devils that scoot through our village, but this cloud is bigger, much bigger. The drone of an engine fills the air. Through the haze, I see metal glinting and a jeep emerges, green and solid, bumping across the rough ground. There are men in the jeep, men with guns.

I haven't seen these men before.

My mouth is dry like dust.

"Kitwana, come back," I call.

The jeep is almost level with Innocence now.

It stops and I see the men talking to her, jabbing their guns into the air.

Time slows down. Innocence spins around. She drops her basket and it falls, the tomatoes exploding on the ground, staining it red, like blood.

And she is running toward us.

Running and running.

And all I can think is that I have never seen Innocence run before. Then she is lost inside the cloud, it swirls around her, swallows her in a burst of sound, cracking like thunder and then we see Innocence falling to the ground.

Falling

Falling

Falling.

But still the cloud of dust moves on, toward us.

"Kitwana, RUN!" I scream.

Kitwana can't move. His legs are rigid and his eyes are wide, wide open. I drop my basket and rush forward and push him toward the scrub. "RUN!"

The jeep is flying across the ground, not slowed by the potholes. The men have seen us.

Big men with guns.

Strong men.

Men who will outrun us.

I see Kitwana running into the scrub, his heels kicking up high behind him. The crackle of gunfire follows him, but I don't see him fall. He's a good runner for his age. The fastest of his friends.

I am running too, my legs pumping across the dirt. The low bushes whip my face and arms.

Maybe Kitwana and I can get away.

I run after him.

But I see him crouching in some bushes, his red T-shirt glaring through the dry leaves and branches.

"Kitwana!" I slap him hard in the face. "I told you to run."

I can hear the thud of heavy boots in the scrub behind us. Kitwana grips me and won't let go. I can see pee trickle down his leg.

"Hide," I order. I grab his hunting knife and shove him deeper into the base of the bush, kicking dry leaves to cover him.

The men are near us now, but I won't let them find Kitwana here.

I turn the other way leading them from Kitwana's hiding place. I run and run, but they are faster than me. I can hear their breath and smell their sweat. I turn and face them, holding Kitwana's knife out in front of me. The big man with the snake-bone bracelet stops as if he can't believe I'm tackling them. A smaller man walks forward and circles me, his hair braided like rats' tails. A smile curls on his lips, amused. He swings his panga around his head like a sword. But I fight first. I plunge my small knife deep in his leg.

The big man laughs out loud, but the rat-haired man's face turns from shock to anger. I see the blade of his panga come singing through the air, cutting a line from my forehead to my chin.

That day, they took me with them.

I learned to hide my heart and keep my tears inside when they opened me up, for the devil to climb in.

CHAPTER THIRTY-NINE

Imara?"

I feel Mama brush away the tears that run down the line of my scar and drip from my chin.

I lean into her, but can't stop the tears from falling.

Mama wraps her arms around me. "Time will heal," she says. "And we have plenty of time."

I want to believe her, but though the scar has healed, the wounds still feel raw. The war still rages deep inside me.

"Come," says Mama. "We have picked enough beans to take to the market."

I follow her back down through the fields. Mama takes me around the back of our hut and shows me a small tree growing in the yard.

"We planted it as a small sapling, the year we lost you," she says.

I reach out to touch the dark shiny leaves. Heavy green fruit hangs from the branches, heart-shaped, sun-blushed with red. "Mangos," I say. "Your favorite."

Mama smiles. "This is the first year it has borne fruit." She picks three mangos and puts two in the basket with the beans for market. "This one's for you," she says, holding out the smallest, ripest mango.

I take it in my hands and feel it soft and ripe beneath my fingers. I don't want to eat it yet. I want to savor its heavy sweetness. I slip it into my pocket and sit down in the cool shadows of the hut. Embe sits next to me, and watches me with her big dark eyes. She looks four, maybe five years old. I wonder what she thinks of me.

"Eat," orders Mama. She hands me a bowl of

sweet potato stew from last night's meal and a strip of cassava bread. It's only as I eat that I remember how hungry I am.

I sit with my back to the hut and watch the road. It's busy with people on their way to market, baskets carried high on their heads, some with goats on tethers trotting by their sides. I begin to remember the road, how it winds through the valley, and then becomes long and straight across a flat plain, passing through more villages until it reaches the town. I remember the town too, the bustle of the open market where women sit beneath striped umbrellas selling their fruit and vegetables.

I need to walk along the road. I need to put what happened there into the past.

Mama takes my bowl, wiped clean with cassava bread. "Are you ready to come with me to market?"

I take a deep breath and nod. I stand up and balance the basket on my head, needing my hand to steady it. "You stay here with Embe, Mama. I can go by myself."

Mama shakes her head. "It is too soon."

I look along the road. "See, it is busy. There are many people on the road today. I won't be alone."

Mama picks at a loose stitch on her sleeve. She glances across at her neighbor, who is piling bananas into a basket. "Maybe I will ask Gladys to walk with you."

I shake my head. "Mama, I need to do this by myself." The truth is I want to walk alone. I feel lonely here among people. Part of me longs for the dark deep green of the forest, for the cool nights and the trailing mists. But I don't let myself think about Kitwana, the young gorilla. I don't go there in my mind. It is my other half-life, and the two halves can never make the whole.

Mama walks with me to the road. "Are you sure you want to do this?"

I nod.

Mama holds me briefly. "Stay close to other people. Once you have finished in the market, come straight home."

I fall in line behind two women with babies strapped around their backs, but they are slower than me, and so I pass them, letting my feet decide the pace. I glance back once to see Mama watching me, clutching Embe's hand.

I try to slide into this new life, carrying beans and mangos to market for Mama. One foot after another. It is the only way forward, I tell myself. I keep up my steady pace until I reach the stretch of long straight road. Ahead of me the road is now empty. I look behind and realize I am on my own. I can't see anyone else at all. I walk faster, striding out, heading for the distance where the road narrows to a point and I can see the beginnings of the town.

The sun is high, high in the sky and the long road is dust dry and hot beneath my feet. The air shimmers in the heat. If I squint, I can almost see through the ripples, like the water of a lake to another life, another time. Ahead I see the place where Innocence fell. I imagine her walking in front of me, her flip-flops slapping on the road, her large bottom swaying side to side, muttering about the two children in her charge. I want to walk with her now. I want to hold her hand. I want to hug her and tell her that my brother got away. I know she was trying to save us.

I wipe the sweat from my eyes. A dust cloud is blowing up. A swirling column of red and yellow filled with the drone of an engine. I see the jeep half hidden in the haze. I blink and blink again and try to see if this is real or in my mind.

But it's very real. My feet feel the throb of the engines through the ground. I can't tell if this is now or then, but I don't feel scared.

I don't feel anything at all.

The jeep keeps on coming, until I am enveloped in its cloud of dust. I close my eyes and sway slightly in the rush of air as it passes. But I hear the brakes screech and it pulls to a stop not far from me. I try to concentrate on the smell of mangos in my basket, the rich sweet scent.

"Imara!"

I try to imagine biting into the rich sticky flesh of mango.

"Imara!"

I open my eyes. A young man is walking toward me, dressed in a green shirt and trousers. A soft green beret sits on his head.

"Imara, I found you."

"Bobo?" I whisper.

Only a few weeks have passed and yet Bobo looks to have grown into a man. "Bobo, is it you?"

We stare at each other in silence while the dust settles around us. Bobo smiles his big wide smile. "May I have one of your sweet mangos?"

I look down at my feet but can't help glancing up at him through my lashes. "I am taking them to market."

Bobo's face falls.

I reach into my pocket and pull out the mango Mama gave me. "But this one is for you."

Bobo runs his fingers across the smooth skin of

the fruit and puts the mango to his nose to breathe in its sweet scent. "Are you well?"

"I am," I say. It's strange seeing him here in front of me.

"Is your family looking after you?"

I pick at the rim of the basket on my head. "They are."

Bobo takes a step toward me. "And you, are you happy?"

I stare at the ground. I feel the silence inside, a wide emptiness.

Bobo opens the door of the jeep and beckons me. "Come with us."

I see the driver of the jeep. He has the same rangers' uniform with the gorilla badge sewn onto his beret.

The man smiles and waves at me. "Hello, Imara. I've heard much about you."

I glance at Bobo.

"This is Kambale, the head ranger of the park," he says.

Kambale grins. "Bobo is our new recruit. He is training to be a ranger like his father, although he has to finish school first."

I climb in and take a seat next to a small boy.

"Imara!"

I spin round to look at him. "Saka, you're here too."

Bobo slides along the seat beside me, and smiles. "Saka is our best tracker."

"But why are you here, Bobo?" I say. "You didn't come just for mangos."

Bobo shakes his head. "We came to find you."

"Why me?" I look between Bobo and Kambale.

"Come," says Kambale. "We will buy your beans and mangos and take you back to your village. And then, Imara, we need to ask for your help. We need you, and Bobo says that no one else will do."

CHAPTER FORTY

I sit outside our hut beneath the shade of dried banana leaves and wait. Mama offers water to Kambale, Bobo, and Saka. Mateso, the village chief, is here too. He closes his eyes and rests his hands on his walking stick as if he has all the time in the world. He's so old, his hair ash white with age and his skin wrinkled, like the bark of a tree. The villagers look to him for his wisdom. I don't remember seeing anyone as old as Mateso in the rebel camp. A group of children have gathered in a semicircle to look at us, and I know the other villagers are watching too. I can see the questions in their eyes. Kitwana and Embe sit with their backs to the hut, pretending they are busy shelling beans, but I know they want to listen. We are all waiting for Babu to come home. The sun drops lower in the sky and the dark shadows slide across the ground. Kambale fidgets with the key to the jeep, keen to return to his home by nightfall.

"He is coming," says Mama.

I look along the road and see the figure of Babu walking toward us. Kitwana jumps and runs to tell him of the visitors, and I see Babu quicken his pace to come to meet us.

Babu nods to Mateso and looks at our visitors.

"Sit down," says Mateso, indicating the wooden stool beside him. "This is Kambale, the head ranger from the national park. He has come to ask for your daughter's help. We have waited for you to be here before we hear what he has to say."

Babu looks between Kambale and me.

Kambale clears his throat. "When Imara was

with the rebels, she looked after a young gorilla, a gorilla she named Kitwana."

I glance across at my brother and see his eyes open wide at his name. A smile plays on Embe's lips and I see her cover her mouth with her hand.

Kambale then says, "She saved the young gorilla and Bobo says she formed a special bond with him, but now the gorilla needs her help."

"Is he sick?" I blurt out.

Mateso frowns at my interruption.

Kambale continues. "He is in our care at the gorilla orphanage, but we can't get him to eat much at all. Kitwana is weakening every day."

The image of him floods into me. I see his arms reaching up for me to carry him. I feel my chest tighten inside.

Mateso puts his hands together beneath his chin. "And you want Imara to go with you and look after this young gorilla?"

Kambale nods.

Mama and Babu are silent, watching and listening.

"For how long?" says Mateso.

Kambale opens his hands out wide. "For as long as she wants."

I feel my world turn upside down.

"The gorilla orphanage needs someone who can care for gorilla babies," says Kambale. "We need someone who understands them."

Babu shakes his head. "Imara is still a child. Where would she stay?"

"She would stay with my family," says Kambale. "We can't pay her, but we will look after her and also send her to school. Then maybe one day she will continue to work with us."

I dig my fingers into the dirt, holding onto the world. I look across at Mama, but can't read her face.

Mateso stands up and walks in a circle around us. "I have seen many things in my lifetime, but not even I can imagine what Imara has been through. She has grown into a woman many years before her age, and we should listen to her wishes. But her mother and father have only just found their child. This is for Imara and her family to decide. Let us leave them to discuss this." He looks to the orange glow of the sun sinking low in the sky and turns to Kambale. "It is too late for you to return to your homes. You can sleep in our village tonight. In the morning, you will know if Imara will be joining you."

When we are alone, Mama takes my hands in hers. "But, Imara, we have only just found you, and now you want to leave us."

"It won't be forever," I say. "I'll come back to visit you."

"But your home is here," says Babu. "Your people are here."

I scratch in the dirt with my toe. "Babu, I see the way the villagers look at me," I say quietly. "They've heard rumors about me. They are wary. They don't trust me. They don't accept me like they did before."

"No," says Mama.

"It's true," I say.

I glance at Babu, but he won't look at me. "I've seen it in your eyes too. I know you want me here with you, but things can never be as they were before. We all know that. You still grieve for the girl you once lost. Part of her is gone forever. I grieve for her too."

Babu takes a deep breath and exhales slowly. "This is where you belong. Your life is here."

I shake my head and try to find the courage to say what I feel. "If I stay, I will be living in the shadows." I look up at him. "Babu, I can't escape my past. I can't escape the things I have seen, but I can decide my future."

Mama takes my hands in hers again and smiles. In the firelight, her eyes shine bright with tears. "What is it *you* want, Imara?"

I squeeze Mama's hands, because I think she will understand. "I saw beautiful things too: the forests, the animals, and the people." I think of the kindness of Frog and his family living on the edges of the park. "One day, I want to be a ranger. Bobo says the park cannot be protected unless the people who live around it are protected too. He says communities need to be involved; they need to be listened to. It was what his father was trying to do. I want to be part of it. It is where I see my future. All our futures."

Mama nods and looks across at Babu. "Well, Babu?"

Babu gets up and walks away from the fire and stands with his back to us, looking out across the dark hills. I join him and stare up at the star-scattered sky. A crescent moon hangs low in the east. In the corral beside us, the cattle stamp and shuffle, getting comfortable for the night.

"Babu?" I say.

I feel his arm around me.

"It was a night like this that I held you for the first time in my arms and gave you your name," he says. "*Imara*. It means *the one who has strength within*. I didn't know then how much you would live up to your name." He pauses, and I feel on the edge of something new, something just out of reach. "You can go," he says, pulling me close to him. "With our blessing."

I lean into him and smile. Even though it's dark, it feels like a bright, bright light is shining deep inside me.

CHAPTER FORTY-ONE

It's a long drive to the orphan gorilla center. I sit between Bobo and Saka and watch the villages and fields pass in a blur until we reach the forests.

"Has Kitwana eaten anything at all?" I ask.

Bobo frowns and stares out the window. "A little, but not much. The vets can't find anything wrong with him, but most of the time he sits in the corner with his arms curled around himself as if he wants to block out the whole world."

I think about all the things he's seen and lost.

It's no wonder that he wants to hide from it all. It's how I have felt too.

"We're here," says Kambale. Saka climbs out to open the gates of the gorilla center, and we drive into the center of the compound. Huge fenced enclosures each hold several gorillas. But these are all big adult gorillas. I look in the trees and on the ground where some are feeding, but I can't see Kitwana here.

Kambale opens the jeep door. "Do you want a drink first?"

I shake my head. All I can think about is Kitwana. Kambale nods. "Come with me."

I follow him with Bobo beside me.

"We have thirteen gorillas here," he says. "Most have been saved from poachers. Some have been rescued from street markets. The local people here help us. We are working with them to protect the edges of the park."

"What will happen to these gorillas?" I ask. "Will they be set free?"

Kambale shakes his head. "They have been in captivity too long, and they know no other life. In some places captive gorillas have been released into the wild, but not here."

Kambale leads us past forested enclosures where the gorillas turn to look at us as we pass. "Kitwana is on his own for now," he says. "We have been keeping him in the quarantine pen."

I feel my heart thumping in my chest as Kambale unlocks the door. Maybe Kitwana won't even recognize me. Maybe he will be too traumatized to come to me.

Kambale hands me a face mask to cover my mouth. "We all wear them to protect the gorillas from human infections," he says. He puts his hand on my back. "Go in," he whispers. "Go and find Kitwana. Let him see you."

I pull the mask over my mouth and slip in through the door. The quarantine pen has four concrete walls and a concrete floor. The staff have added large branches for climbing and an old tire for Kitwana to swing from, but all I see is Kitwana huddled in the corner of the room, his back to the world. He is swaying back and forth, back and forth.

I step closer and crouch down behind him. "Kitwana!" I whisper.

I see his body become still. He holds his breath but doesn't turn around.

"Kitwana!" I call, louder this time.

He turns and looks at me, his amber eyes finding mine.

I hold out my arms and watch him shuffle over, slowly at first, sniffing the air as if he doesn't quite believe what he is seeing. Then he reaches up and wraps his arms around me, gripping me with his fingers and toes, as he pulls himself close. I wrap my arms around him and we stay like that, holding on to each other, neither of us wanting to let go.

Kambale crouches next to me. "Why don't you and Bobo take Kitwana for a walk into the forest? Let him play for a while. Let him find some food."

I nod and walk with Bobo. Kitwana releases his

tight grip on me, and lets Bobo take his other hand. Bobo is silent as we walk through the trees, swinging Kitwana between us. Sunlight reaches down, casting deep shadows on the forest floor. We stop beside a fallen tree and let Kitwana scramble over the twisted roots. I lean against the trunk and watch him play. He doesn't go far, and keeps glancing back at me to make sure that I'm still there. I feel the hot sun and the damp scent of the forest. I don't want to leave Kitwana again. I want to stay in this moment. I want it to last forever. Kitwana comes back with a handful of leaves and twigs and sits beside me, chewing them and tearing strips of soft bark from the woody stems.

"He's eating." I smile.

Bobo sits back against a tree root and folds his hands behind his head. "Is this what you want, Imara?"

I nod and reach out for Kitwana. I run my fingers beneath his armpits and tickle him. He squirms beneath my hands and wrinkles his nose in pleasure. "This is where I belong, here, with Kitwana."

"What about leaving your family, your village?" says Bobo.

I put my hand to cover my scar. "What future would I have there, Bobo? I am not the girl they remember. Who would want me?"

Bobo sits up and takes my hand in his. "Look at me."

I don't want to look. I don't want his pity.

But Bobo takes my other hand. "Imara, look at me."

I turn and don't see pity in his eyes, just truth.

"I see you, Imara," he says, "and you are beautiful, to me."

Kambale is waiting for us in the quarantine pen with some fresh leaves for Kitwana. I tear some and pretend to chew them to encourage Kitwana to eat.

Kambale watches me. "I'm glad that you came to work with us. Bobo was right; you have a natural way with gorillas."

I look up at Kambale and smile. "This way I get to look after Kitwana, too." I push my fingers through his fur. "I don't want to lose him again."

I see Bobo and Kambale exchange glances. Bobo stares down at his hands and won't look me in the eye.

"What is it?" I ask.

"There are many young gorillas who will need your help," says Kambale. "But not Kitwana."

I wrap my arms around Kitwana. "What d'you mean?"

Bobo shuffles next to me. "It's only been five weeks since Kitwana was taken from his family. Kambale thinks we should try to reunite them."

I turn to Kambale. "What if the other gorillas don't want him?"

Kambale takes a deep breath. "We think it is worth the risk. It is important to have as many gorillas in the wild as we can. Kitwana could grow to be a silverback one day, with a family of his own."

"But so soon?" I say. "You said he hasn't been eating."

"If we return him now, his mother may still have milk to feed him."

I shake my head and hold Kitwana tight against me. "But what if the other gorillas kill him first?"

Kambale nods. "It is a risk, but Enzi the black-back is still young. Usually it's the silverbacks that kill babies that are not their own. Enzi is not a silverback yet. He has grown up with Kitwana. I think he will accept him back."

"So why bring me here now?" I ask.

It's Bobo who answers. "Kitwana trusts you. We need you to come with us and carry Kitwana to his family. He won't go with anyone but you."

"And what if we don't find his family?" I say, half hoping.

"We know where they are," says Kambale. "We have rangers watching them right now."

Kitwana curls his fingers around my neck, sensing my fear. Now that I've found him, I don't want to let him go. "Then when?" I ask. "When do we release him?"

"It is best to try as soon as possible," says Kambale. "He will thrive better with his family."

I look between Kambale and Bobo. "When?"

"Tomorrow," says Bobo. "We release him tomorrow, in the forest, at dawn."

CHAPTER FORTY-TWO

It is time, Imara."

When Bobo wakes me, I try to pull my blanket over my head and fall back into sleep. Kitwana is next to me, his body curled into mine. His breathing is slow and steady, and his fingers twitch in his sleep. I want to keep him next to me. He's the missing part of me. I don't want to let him go.

"Imara," whispers Bobo, "it is time to go."

I get dressed and wrap Kitwana in my blanket, carrying him with me to the waiting jeep. Kitwana half wakes as the jeep rumbles to life, then falls asleep again as he feels me next to him. It's two hours until dawn. The night is absolute. The headlights shine out into the darkness, picking out the dirt road and the potholes sliding beneath us. We drive blindly through the night. We could be anywhere, anywhere at all.

Kambale speaks into the radio to the rangers in the forest who have been camped near the Tumaini group, and we stop on a forest track, an hour's hike away.

I follow Bobo and the other rangers into the forest. I feel Kitwana shift in my arms, and although I can't see him, I'm sure he's awake, watching and listening. I feel his fingers cling to my arms. We move in the predawn darkness, with head flashlights lighting the way along a path cut by the rangers the day before. The path winds steeply up and up. I inhale the scent of the forest and feel the cool mist touching my bare shoulders. My muscles burn with tiredness, yet it feels good to be back here. It feels good to be alive.

The darkness melts and the sky above turns a deep leaf-patterned blue. We walk and walk, until the forest opens out onto a small clearing on a ridge. To one side lies the forest reaching upward toward the top of the mountain, and on the other, we have a view down across the rest of the forest, the dense canopy of leaves spreading across the land like a soft dark blanket. A pale mist clings to the treetops. In the east, beams of sunlight reach up from the horizon and the sky glows orange with the promised sun.

"Shh!" whispers Kambale from ahead. "We are here. Keep Kitwana out of sight until I say."

I wrap the blanket around Kitwana, but I can't help moving forward to see the gorillas. In the pale dawn light, I can see their dark shapes waking from their night's sleep. Enzi is first to wake, hearing us arrive. He lifts his head and stares in our direction. Then he sits up, stretching his arms and he yawns, his lips peeling back to show huge canine teeth; teeth that could rip Kitwana apart.

The females begin to stir, pulling twigs and branches from their makeshift nests and chewing on the tough leaves.

Bobo nudges me and points to a gorilla a little way from the others, still curled in sleep. "That's Kitwana's mother."

I hold Kitwana tightly against me and watch her. She's not asleep. She's lying with her eyes open, her arms curled around her chest as if holding onto the shape of something lost. She sits up and moves with a slow listlessness, keeping herself away from the others.

"She's lost weight," says Kambale. "She has not been the same since losing Kitwana and the silverback."

Another female stirs.

"That's Heri," says Bobo. He stands up to get a better view. His eyes open wider and wider. "Kambale, why didn't you tell me?"

Kambale chuckles and points to the tiny gorilla baby cradled in Heri's arms. "I thought I would leave it a surprise for you. She had her baby gorilla girl two nights ago."

I peer over Bobo's shoulder and see the tiny baby feeding from her mother.

"I'm going to move a little closer," says Kambale.

Bobo and I stand with the other rangers and watch Kambale step forward, making the low grunting noises to calm Enzi and let him know we are not a threat.

"The gorillas know Kambale," whispers Bobo. "He and my father have been following this group for years. They are used to people. It is good, because the tourists are slowly returning to see the gorillas."

Kambale gives a series of grunts. I feel Kitwana wriggle to look beyond me and I try to keep him out of sight. Kambale wants to assess the group first, but Kitwana tries to pull away from me. He sniffs the air and grasps my shoulders to look over at the gorilla group through the trees. I try to crouch to hide him, but Kitwana hoots and there is nothing I can do to stop him.

Enzi stiffens and looks in our direction.

Kitwana hoots again.

"Move back," urges Kambale. He flaps his hands at me.

I move back into the forest but Enzi is alert, his mouth drawn into a tight pout. He moves toward us, and stands with his body sideways to us, showing off his huge domed head and muscled back and arms.

Kambale is waving me back. "We must leave slowly," he says in hushed whispers. "This is not good. Enzi has taken control. This may not be good for Kitwana."

I move back, but Enzi is pushing his way through the vines.

Kambale shakes his head. "I have made a mistake."

Bobo tries to stand between Enzi and me, shielding me from view, but Enzi will be too strong. Kambale has his rifle close, but I know he doesn't want to use it.

"Back . . . back . . . back!" urges Kambale, but Enzi keeps coming, pushing his way through the vines toward us. The other gorillas are awake and watching from a distance, huddled in a group.

The rangers stand back and let him pass. Enzi sees Kitwana. He stops and sniffs the air. Kitwana hoots and tries to pull away from me, but I hold him close.

Enzi stands up tall and thumps his chest; the hollow pok-poks of his chest-beats echo in the forest.

"Put Kitwana down," warns Kambale. "Walk away."

"He'll kill him," I whisper.

"It is too dangerous for you to stay. Leave him," warns Kambale.

But I won't let Enzi kill him.

"Put him down," orders Kambale.

Kitwana can sense the danger. He clutches me. I start backing away through the forest, but Enzi is coming. He pushes past the rangers, the vines snapping and cracking beneath his feet. I can smell the musty scent of his alarm.

"Imara, put Kitwana on the ground and leave him!" Kambale shouts in panic.

But I hold Kitwana and stand my ground.

Enzi rises up on his legs and beats his fists against his chest again. I glare up at him. He's taller than me, almost twice as tall. I look him directly in the eye; I know it's a challenge, but I won't let Kitwana die.

Enzi drops to his arms and charges in full roar. It's so fast. All I see is a blur of black, and his mouth wide open, his huge canines filling the space.

"Let go!" screams Bobo.

But I can't let go. I cling to Kitwana. Enzi thumps me in the chest. It's a blow so powerful it takes my breath away and for a moment I lose hold of Kitwana and fall back onto the ground. As I lie there I see Enzi dragging Kitwana away by his foot, his small body bumping on the ground after him.

I scramble to my feet, sucking air into my chest. I try to follow, but Bobo holds me back.

"He'll kill him," I say.

"There's nothing we can do. If you try to get Kitwana, Enzi might kill you, too."

I hold on to a vine and watch. I can't breathe.

Enzi lifts Kitwana by the leg, dangling him in the air while he snuffs and pokes him with his long finger. Kitwana is limp. He just hangs from Enzi's hand, his eyes open, watching.

The rest of the group has crowded around, intent on exploring the new gorilla. Enzi drops Kitwana to the ground where he lies unmoving. He's so still, I wonder if his neck is broken.

Then I see Kitwana's mother push her way forward. She stops in front of Enzi, her huge body tensed. She just stares at Kitwana, her nose sniffing the air trying to get the scent of him. Deep furrows line her forehead. She moves closer and sits beside Kitwana, putting herself between him and Enzi. She reaches down and pulls her baby up into her arms, wrapping them around him, protecting him. She pushes her face into his fur, smelling him,

holding him. I see his small arm uncurl and reach up to his mother and they just stare deep, deep, deep into each other's eyes, their faces almost touching.

The other gorillas crowd around, but Hisani has her son back again and holds him close. I try to get a better view, but Enzi stands between his family and the rangers. This is his family and he won't let us near again. He urges them to move away from us, pushing them up into the forest.

I catch one last glimpse of Kitwana, clutching his mother, looking out on the world. He looks right at me, right into my eyes. It's so fleeting. A brief moment snatched in this predawn light, yet it holds me. I feel it long after Kitwana and his mother have slipped away into the shadows between the trees.

Kitwana is with his family where he belongs.

And I feel no sorrow, and no sadness, only joy.

Pure joy.

I turn to look at Bobo, but for the first time, I see his face is wet with tears.

"What is it, Bobo?"

Bobo doesn't answer at first. He wipes the tears on his sleeve and shakes his head.

"Bobo? Aren't you happy? Kitwana is with his family. He is free."

He stares into the forest. "But for how long, Imara? How long can they survive? We know what it's like. We have seen it. The Black Mamba and the White Lioness will not be the last ones here. The world won't stop until it has destroyed everything and taken what's beneath our soil."

Kambale puts his hand on Bobo's shoulder. "And that is why we are here," he says, "to stop it from happening."

"But who will listen?" Bobo kicks the ground. "My father died for the animals and people here. But it made no difference. No one cares."

Kambale holds Bobo by the shoulders. "Your father was a brave man. He gave his life, because he never gave up hope."

Bobo stares down at his father's beret, turning it

over and over in his hands, watching his tears make dark spots on the green fabric. "You're right," he says softly. He wipes his sleeve across his face and stands up tall. He pulls the beret onto his head and nods. "You're right. My father never gave up hope. His last words were ones of courage. They give me strength to go on."

I take Bobo's hand. "Then tell me," I say, "so I can find his courage too."

Bobo turns his face to the golden rim of sun brimming above the horizon. He takes a deep breath. "Imara, what do you see?"

I squint into the light. "I see the sun rising above the mountain."

Bobo repeats the words of his father, the words that have now become his own.

"Close your eyes and feel the whole *world* turn beneath your feet. As it turns, we turn with it. You and me . . . we are all part of it. Everything we are, everything we do connects us with it.

"Breathe this air.

"Drink this rain.

"The earth pulses with the life it gives us.

"But if we lose our love of it, then we lose everything. But most of all, we lose ourselves. We lose our souls.

"So, what gives me the right to sit back and do nothing to protect it? With every dawn, I ask myself: Who am I? What is my part in this? How am I going to use *this* day, to make the next one a better world?"

gorilla

Kitwana clings to his mother, remembering the sway of her body, feeling her strong arm around him. The forest wraps itself around them both, drawing them in, protecting them beneath its canopy. Kitwana rides on his mother's back, as Enzi leads them farther up the mountain.

When Enzi stops to feed, the other gorillas crowd around Kitwana. Wary of him at first, they sniff their noses into the air, taking in the scent of Tall Apes on him. Kitwana's mother won't let them close yet. She barks when they try to touch him.

Enzi watches them all and sits next to Kitwana's mother

for her to groom him. She doesn't look Enzi in the eye, but keeps an arm around her son. She begins to groom Enzi with her fingers, releasing her grip on Kitwana as she picks through Enzi's fur. Kitwana joins her, raking his small fingers across Enzi's skin.

The other gorillas settle, seeing Enzi has accepted Kitwana back. They feed and rest together. Sunlight reaches down into the twilight world beneath the canopy. Kitwana clambers in the trees and spins on the thick lianas that drape across the forest. For a while, Enzi forgets he is the head of the family and chases Kitwana round and round, playing the games he played before, with Kitwana shrieking in delight.

This is how Kitwana remembers his family.

He feels safe, protected.

This is his world.

For now.

As the day draws into night, Kitwana curls up with his mother in the nest of leaves she has wrapped around them. He rests his head against her chest and listens to her soft breathing and the steady beat of her heart. Slowly, his eyes begin to close.

Sleep finds him cradled next to his mother, hidden in night's deep shadows.

Above, the moon traces its bright arc across the sky.

The constellations spin.

And the whole world turns toward a new tomorrow.

Dear Reader,

The idea for *Gorilla Dawn* was sparked by an article that linked mobile phones to the fate of gorillas. Intrigued, I read on to discover that many of the minerals used in the manufacture of mobile phones and other electronic devices are sourced in the Democratic Republic of Congo, home of the eastern lowland gorilla. One of the minerals, tantalum, is found in the ore coltan, which is extracted by hand from open mines, often constructed within the forest home of the gorillas. Huge areas of forests are being destroyed for mining, logging, and charcoal production. And not only are the gorillas under threat from habitat loss, but also from poaching for bush meat and the illegal pet trade, and from diseases such as Ebola.

Gorilla Dawn is set in the Democratic Republic of Congo, a country abundant in wildlife and minerals. But despite its natural riches, it is one of the poorest countries in the world, due to the exploitation of its people and resources. World greed for resources has funded various rebel groups and corrupt army officials to continue the instability. Recent history has seen huge political unrest. Since the outbreak of fighting in the 1990s, over five million people have died as a result of the violence. It has been the deadliest conflict since World War II.

The forests are vital for the people who live near them and for those of us who live thousands of miles away.

The Equatorial rainforests drive our weather patterns around the world and regulate our climate. The forests are not a benign paradise; they are essential to all life on earth.

And yet, time is running out, especially for the gorillas.

A report commissioned by the United Nations Environment Program in 2010 estimates that only 10% of the gorilla habitat will remain by 2032. Even this is thought to be optimistic. The eastern lowland gorilla may face extinction before 2050. If this happens, it would be a huge loss for us all.

However, there is hope. The numbers of mountain gorillas in the Virunga National Park have been increasing slowly as a result of conservation strategies working within the forests and with local communities. There are also many brave men and women rangers who risk their lives on a daily basis to protect the forests and the animals.

Our own fate and that of the gorillas are bound together. Our everyday actions have ramifications far across the globe. Yet, this gives us power, knowing that what we can do as individuals can really make a difference.

"You cannot get through a single day without having an impact on the world around you. What you do makes a difference, and you have to decide what kind of difference you want to make."—Jane Goodall

Gill Lewis–2015

Gill Lewis is the author of the critically acclaimed novels *Wild Wings* and *One White Dolphin*, both winners of the Green Earth Book Award, as well as *Moon Bear*. As a veterinarian, her love for animals and the natural world plays a big part in her writing. She lives in the United Kingdom.